NEIGHBOURS & TOURISTS

Neighbours & Tourists

A collection of short stories

by

EWA MAZIERSKA

Adelaide Books
New York / Lisbon
2019

NEIGHBOURS & TOURISTS
A collection of short stories
By Ewa Mazierska

Published by Adelaide Books, New York / Lisbon
adelaidebooks.org

Editor-in-Chief
Stevan V. Nikolic

For any information, please address Adelaide Books
at info@adelaidebooks.org
or write to:
Adelaide Books
244 Fifth Ave. Suite D27
New York, NY, 10001

ISBN-10: 1-950437-73-6
ISBN-13: 978-1-950437-73-3

Printed in the United States of America

Contents

PART 1: NEIGHBOURS

The Death of a Neighbour

We called our neighbours by their surnames; this was a custom in our village. Those who came from outside, even if only a neighbouring village and settled among us, were described as 'T.'s wife' or 'K.'s husband'; these people rarely gained an identity of their own. We had closer and further neighbours; this pointed less to their physical proximity to our house, more the neighbourly ties, reflected in paying each other small favours and exchanging gossip. However, the closer neighbours kept dying. Currently on our street we had two houses which were unoccupied, including one with a 'For Sale' sign. My mother found it outrageous, as for the last 60 or so years there had never been any house for sale in our neighbourhood, People built houses and then passed them on to their offspring. But now the children did not want or could not stay in the village, even if they had a property there. The deaths of the neighbours inevitably affected the hierarchy of those who remained; the further ones by virtue of being still around moved to the position of the close ones. This is what happened some years ago to the Szs.: Bronek Sz. and Sz.'s wife. They were not considered close neighbours by my mother till some years ago, when the houses between our house and theirs were left empty. That said, we were always on good terms with them and when my granny was still alive, she exchanged with them seeds and plants, as Bronek was an avid gardener, as was my granny. Now he was the last such gardener on our street, having in his garden-cum-orchard a full set of vegetables and fruit, including tomatoes, gooseberries and white currants, which by this point had disappeared not only from our neighbourhood, but the whole region. The Szs. were also the last to keep hens, ducks and geese, and my mother were buying eggs from them. I liked Bronek very much and my sympathy was reciprocated. Whenever I came home in summer, he would say 'Our princess has returned and brought good weather.' Bronek also usually asked me how things were 'in the wide world' or 'what people in the world think about Polish people', to which I always replied that things are getting better and people in the world have a very high opinion of Poles. I wasn't sure if I answered truly, but Bronek was an optimist and a patriot and there was no point to undermine his mindset.

To reciprocate, I asked him how things were in the village, to which he replied listing deaths and births of people, whose names were mostly unfamiliar to me. He also invited me to his garden, where I collected large quantities of fruit because, as he complained, there were too much of them for him and his wife. Sometimes Bronek's wife went out, said 'hello' and remarked that the weather was good, but I never had any lengthy discussions with her, partly on account of the fact that she was just Bronek's wife, rather than a 'native' and partly because she wanted to keep her distance. Maybe the reason was that she was not from our village but from far away (meaning from another side of the nearby town of Włocławek) or maybe she felt embarrassed by her position. Apparently she'd graduated from a technical college and had held a position of authority in a wire factory in Włocławek, till she lost it, either because the factory was downsized or due to an alcohol problem and absenteesm. The truth was that the Szs. liked alcohol, although they were not typical village drunkards, found lying semi-conscious on park benches or engaged in arguments with other drunkards. They drank behind closed doors, just the two of them and not every day, and they did not drink the cheapest fruit wine or cheap vodka purchased in the local shops, but their own, home-made fruit brandy. They did not have close ties with other people in the village, perhaps because they were a childless couple and such couples are usually more attached to each other and self-sufficient than couples with children.

All our talks and businesses with the Szs. were conducted in the courtyard, their garden or on the pavement near their house. Although my mother was nosy, on such occasions she preferred not to know how the interior of their house looked, being worried that she might embarrass them during their drinking sessions or be put off herself by the dirt or disorder she might find there. 'It is better not to know how the alcoholics live,' she used to say. But last summer, during my Polish vacation, we had an opportunity to visit the Szs. in their home. Indeed, it was more than an opportunity – a moral duty, caused by the death of Bronek's wife. Paradoxically, only then she became promoted from being Bronek's wife to Irena and her life as an individual came under scrutiny. It was established that she died of breast cancer, an illness usually curable when early detected. For my mother, who never missed an opportunity to have a medical test, the fact that Irena did not have an appropriate examination till it was too late was a sign of her backwardness. Another conclusion she drew from Irena's death was that our village was cursed by cancer; all our neighbours who'd recently passed away died from this illness.

Death in our village required neighbours to visit the houses of the deceased a day before the funeral with flowers, candles and prayers, to facilitate their road to heaven. As a teenager, I boycotted such celebrations, finding them backward and in disagreement with my ostentatious atheism, but now I was happy to join in and even become a believer. It seemed to be possible, The mechanical repetition of the Rosary, singing religious hymns and smelling funerals flowers, specially chosen to overcome the smell of the corpse, quickly decomposing in the warm weather, put me in a semi-religious mood. I almost felt like there exists some heaven, where souls are floating and embracing each other, in the same way as we, the neighbours, embraced each other in our grief and the sense of fragility of our own mortal coil. My impromptu religiosity was appreciated by Bronek and the other neighbours, even more so, as the tradition of visiting the deceased before their funeral was also dying. One neighbour noticed that when my father died almost thirty years ago, there were over a hundred people who came for the prayer – more than our house could accommodate. This time there were only fourteen and all of them were old; I was the second youngest and I also recently turned fifty.

The interior of the Szs.' house looked better than we expected, perhaps because it was specially prepared for the funeral. It occurred to me, however, that it also reflected on Bronek's wife's sense of taste, which persisted despite the Szs's relatively poor and alcohol-fuelled existence. There were quite a lot of books, mainly the classics of Polish literature, the Mickiewiczs and the Słowackis, which haunted me during my school years and now filled my heart with sadness, like the flowers and prayers. There was some old furniture made of solid wood, of the type my mother disposed of in the seventies in her drive to modernise our house, following the last attempt to modernise Poland during socialism. There were also some crystal vases and bowls which were so old that they looked more vintage than kitsch. Next to the room with Irena's corpse there were snacks for the guests: sandwiches and cakes, brought by the neighbours, but they were barely touched. The day was too hot to eat; we were only drinking mineral water.

Bronek did not appear heartbroken or even sad, but energetic, as if everything he had in mind was to ensure that the ceremony went well. This was only natural because people who are truly heartbroken do not need to show it. Moreover, it must have been a challenge for him to organise such a complex event, given that he led such a quiet and simple life. He stood up to the occasion. Both the prayers in his home went well and the atmosphere was almost cheerful in the end, as well as nostalgic, as people were reminiscing on other neighbours who had died recently. The funeral the next day was also touching, although again few people came and the ceremony was led by a young priest, new to the job. Maybe because of that he came across as free of pomposity for which the local rector was widely known and mildly despised. The priest said that true love is a great rarity, and the Szs., who were married for almost thirty years, were blessed with it. This would ensure Bronek's serenity even when his wife was laid to rest in her grave. My mother shed tears when he said that, perhaps realising that she'd not been blessed with such love and, indeed, nobody in our family had been. Surprisingly, there was no talk of a reunion in heaven or the need to pay for extra church services to prevent Irena from descending into hell.

'What will happen now to Bronek?' I asked my mother on our way home.

'He will drink himself to death,' she replied. 'What's life worth to him now, when he has nobody to share it with?' she asked rhetorically.

I was on the verge of saying that it hadn't been the case with her when her husband died, but I resisted the temptation, knowing that such a statement would not be taken lightly by her. On this occasion my mother was in agreement with was what other neighbours were saying about the widower. Then it turned out that they were not entirely right, as I learnt when I bumped into Bronek when cycling to the shop. He stopped me and we had a chat, first about the funeral, which he pronounced had been 'very much to Irena's taste,' and then about Bronek's future life. As if trying to pre-empt people's expectations, he admitted to having no desire to die yet. His life might be more difficult now, but it was still worth living, when there is a small plot of land to attend to and some animals to look after. He also confessed that he had little faith in the posthumous life in the normal sense – dead people only live as long as they live in other people's memory. Therefore when he died, Irena would die for the second time. He wanted to live a bit longer for her, at least to make sure that their gravestone was erected and all inheritance issues properly taken care of.

This was my last meeting with Bronek. Less than a week later I returned to Britain and several months later he was diagnosed with cancer, dying before my next visit to Poland. On this occasion I was glad that I missed the common prayers as I'd have found the occasion too mournful. When I returned, I noticed a 'For Sale' sign in front of Bronek's house. There was a particular stillness about the house, given that before it was so noisy, with ducks and geese cackling and dog barking. Apparently as soon as Bronek died, somebody came and took all the birds, but the dog remained, as nobody wanted it. Eventually somebody arrived from the mayor's office and took him to the shelter in Włocławek, so that the neighbours weren't left with the dirty work of disposing of him. Last time when I passed Bronek's house with my mother, she said with her typical drama, 'soon our entire village will be deserted.'

Too Smart

My grandma used to say 'It is not worth being too smart.' These words come to my mind when I'm thinking about the Ns., who were our closest neighbours, living on the opposite side of the road, slightly to the right of our house. They were also close to us socially, so to speak. The N. used to come to discuss political issues with my father and his wife used to visit my grandmother to exchange cooking recipes for cakes and jams. She was also keen to borrow small sums of money, which she used to repay in a week or two. I always considered the Ns. funny. He was funny on account of his loud voice; she due to being fat, short and extremely energetic. Later I also learnt that they had funny names: Teodor and Teofila, which for me suited better animals in the children television programmes than real people.

The Ns. lived in a large house with a huge orchard and courtyard, and plenty of sheds. However, they were not farmers, as there was no field behind their house and I never saw Teodor driving a horse cart or a tractor to a field outside the village. But then I do not remember any of them having a regular job either. Irrespective of the season Teodor used to work around his house and Teofila was busy in the kitchen or visited neighbours to spread gossip. When recently, for the sake of writing their story, I consulted my mother about

Teodor's job, she told me that he was on incapacity benefit. This might have surprised a stranger, given that Teodor was always moving a huge amount of wood around his house or building a shed, sporting an athletic figure, but during the communist times almost half of men in our village were on incapacity benefit. The second half were farmers, who could not get incapacity benefit even if they were sick. The smart people tried to move from full-time employment to incapacity benefit as soon as possible so that they could engage in better paid work or devote their lives to acquiring shortage goods. Apparently the three mansions the local doctors built for themselves and their children were paid by fake certificates about incapacity of the local people. But let's return to the Ns. Making sure he was not short of shortage goods was Teodor's favourite occupation. Getting what was difficult to get was everybody's ambition, but Teodor went in this respect further that anybody else. The peak of his thrift was during the martial law in the early 1980s when the contents of the Polish shops were transferred wholesale to people's pantries, leaving only vinegar and tins of squid imported from the Soviet Union boxes on the shelves. During this time my parents amassed over twenty kilos of sugar and flour. But Teodor looked at our supplies with disdain, confessing that of sugar alone he had 200 kilos. As for flour, tea and dry sausage he was not sure, but if a war of the length of the Second World War was to start the next day, the Ns. had enough food supplies to keep them going till its end. They had also plenty of coal and wood. It filled all the sheds in the courtyard and when there was no more space for wood in the sheds and for sheds to be built, Teodor used part of his house as storage. I think it was around this time that my grandma described the Ns. as too smart. Too smart for their own good – this was what she meant.

For Teodor food did not mean the pleasures of cooking and eating, or at best they were of secondary importance to him. Food meant fuel. Therefore he liked most what was rich in energy: meat, bread, potatoes and deplored everything which was too fancy. Adding spices was for him like polluting petrol. Teofila tried to process the excessive food acquired by her husband, hence her constant baking of cakes, jam-making and rolling dough for dumplings. I still remember the taste of her layered cakes and redcurrant jam. In exchange, my mother, who worked in a local chemist shop, kept bringing her medicines for indigestion.

It would be a literary achievement to come up with a theory explaining Teodor's hoarding obsession, for example to discover that he was a concentration camp prisoner who suffered from long-time hunger and cold, but unfortunately it was not the case. He suffered no more than ordinary inhabitants of our village and many people would say that the Ns. got a better life than most of us. This was because they benefitted from good connections. Teodor's brother was a local Party dignitary and Teofila's sister lived in West Germany. While the advantages of the first connection was difficult to measure, the second was obvious. The Ns.' daughters used to wear western clothes and Teofila had various kitchen appliances which provided a discord to her otherwise old-fashioned and poorly maintained kitchen. She even passed on to us one or two foreign items, but they turned out as useless for us as they were for them, proving that everyday life is a system; one cannot change one element without moving many others.

Teodor and Teofila had two daughters. I was never friends with them, because being seven and nine years older than me, they belonged to a different generation, but I liked them. The older, Ela, had a very loud voice, like her father and was joyful, tall and pretty. The younger, Lidia, spoke quietly and was rather mousy. The only remarkable thing about her was that she was a heavy smoker; she started early and must have smoked two packets of cigarettes per day as she seemed to always have a cigarette in her mouth. Maybe because of that she couldn't find a husband, which greatly worried Teofila. At the time spinsterhood was seen as a pretty grim predicament. It was a great relief for her mother when Lidia got herself a boyfriend as she was over thirty by then.

I'm not sure when the lives of the Ns. took a turn for the worse. Perhaps it was after the fire, in the early 1980s. The fire broke in their courtyard and did not damage their house, only destroyed some sheds and wood laying loose in front of them. But afterwards people started to point to the Ns. the danger of having so much fuel around their house. Even a local fire inspector told them that if they did not comply with the health and safety regulations, they would face hefty penalties. Some things indeed changed, as was later discovered. Teodor, without giving up his wood and coal, switched to a 'smarter' form of energy by diverting the stream of electrons aimed to the house-holds of his neighbours to his own house. This operation, in which Teodor was assisted by his son-in-law, was initially very successful as proved by the fact that the Ns.' electricity bill shrank to zero. However, the trick ultimately frustrated Teodor, as he was unable to hoard electricity – what he stole he had to use on the spot. Moreover, another inspector came to check why there were electric lights in their house while, according to their electricity bill, the Ns. lived like cavemen.

These brushes with the law drove a wedge between Teodor and his apparatchik brother. The brother did not want his rep-utation to be tarnished by a connection to a criminal. Teodor, being a man of an independent mind (as he liked to present himself), not only ignored his brother's warnings to use energy like everybody else, but got more defiant. His sheds got higher and more elaborate, more like fortresses than sheds, and there was a sign of a bunker being dug in the Ns.' orchard. Somebody on our road even named the Ns.' adobe 'little Albania'. For a time this name stuck and when people said it, they pointed to their foreheads, indicating that the inhabitants of this place were not healthy of mind. Teodor did not care. His next project was a small chapel to the Holy Mary in his front garden. Later on a chapel of this kind would also appear in the garden of the Bs., but in the case of the Bs.. it was a reflection of their true religiosity; in the case of the Ns. of spite towards Teodor's brother. On this occasion he again proved 'too smart', because by the mid-1980s religiosity started to be seen not as a handicap, but as a way to save one's public life. In due course Teodor's brother claimed that he was always a good Catholic, as proved by his brother's private chapel towards which he contributed financially.

The final blow to Teodor came in the 1990s, when the economy of shortages finished in Poland and money became the only thing people were short of. He still had some hope that the domestic and world politics would turn to his advantage and at times the world appeared to move in his direction. Every closed down Polish coalmine was like honey to his mouth, as it meant less coal for a Pole. Teodor also looked with hope at the rise of Islamic fundamentalism in the Arab countries, predicting that it would lead to cutting oil supplies to the West. Russia also would eventually say 'no' to the persecution of Russians in its old republics and at a minimum would invade Ukraine, which would reduce oil stream coming to Poland. Furthermore, there might be a conflict between Poland and Germany as, after all, Poland stole a large chunk of its neighbour's territory in 1945. All these developments were meant to leave Poland isolated and cut off from energy supplies, giving Teodor an advantage. His prophecies, however, were increasingly a subject of jokes in the village.

By mid-1990s both daughters of the Ns. were married and the older left the family home to live with her husband and two children in the regional capital of Włocławek. Since then she was rarely seen in our neighbourhood. The younger stayed in her parents' house and in due course also had two children. However, by the time the younger child was born, Lidia's husband disappeared. The common belief was that he was a drunkard and a crook, who eventually ended up in prison. People even wondered if it wouldn't be better for her to be a spinster rather than having a husband good for nothing. As the first decade of democracy progressed, Teofila was losing her energy. She got diabetes and stayed indoors more and more. From being a chief disseminator of gossip, she was downgraded to its recipient. Teodor fared even worse, as in his older age he got all the illnesses he faked in his young age to get incapacity benefit. He lost his strength, he got back pain and his heart was failing him. He could not build any more sheds or even mend those which needed repair. He was also constantly harassed by the police, even when he was bed-ridden.

But the misfortune which befell the Ns. was small in comparison with that of their daughters who died before reaching forty; the older from colon cancer and the younger from lung cancer. Although people in our village were neither particularly superstitious nor profound, they saw a connection between their deaths and the sins of their parents. This is because cancer is a reaction to excess, for having too much to burn: food in the case of Ela's cancer and fuel in Lidia's. Teodor, being metaphorically and literally deaf, made nothing of such comments, but Teofila took them to heart. However, she had little time to ponder on her guilt, as she had to look after Lidia's children. The alternative was an orphanage, as their father was behind bars and wasn't interested in them anyway. Teofila's main objective was to survive till her granddaughter, Joanna, reached seventeen, as by then not only would she be too old to be taken into care, but she could become her younger brother's legal guardian. Teofila died five months after her husband and two weeks after Joanna's seventeenth birthday. Her funeral attracted a sizeable crowd. Although people remembered Teofil's eccentricity and criminality, in the hour of his wife's death what was remembered was only that they were one of 'us'.

Focusing on preserving one's physical existence, as was the case in the Ns' last years, made everything else decline at an accelerated rate. The house got more hunched every time I visited our village, the wood in the courtyard was rotting, the Holy Mary in the chapel lost an eye and her blue heart, and their dogs roamed the streets, howling and attacking the cyclists, as if they were strays.

It was very difficult for Joanna to lose all her family, although the blow was cushioned by certain advantages. She inherited some money from her great-aunt, the one who lived in Germany and got compensation for losing a part of their garden when a motorway was built nearby. She had money to live on for some years and even to sort out some of the problems around the house. But this I know only from my mother, as when Joanna was a child, I was already living abroad. In fact, I did not even know how she looked. Hence, I was surprised when during one of my summer visits, she came round, bringing a bucket of black currants. She said she did not know what to do with all the fruit growing in the orchard and it occurred to her that we might want to use them for jam. Her granny told her that my grandma's jam was the best on our street. Joanna did not look anything like her grandparents or her mother, so it was almost a shock for me to think that she came from the same family. She was a very blond, slim and pretty girl, but seemed to be a bit shy.

I invited Joanna to the kitchen, and she was happy to sit, drink tea, smoke cigarettes and tell me about herself. She confirmed that her life was hard, but not only because her relatives were dead or in prison, but also because she was not smart. She had a problem learning new things, failed twice her driving test and was not sure if she would pass her A-levels. The ultimate proof of her not being smart was that she was stuck in the village, like the old people, while almost everybody else of the working age left, for England, Germany or at least Warsaw.

'You also must have been smart to move to England and even do so before everybody,' she finished her autobiography.

For a while I did not know what to say and then asked, 'do you know how to make jam?'

'I do,' said Joanna. 'Cherry, plum, redcurrant, blackcurrant, even apple. I can bring some for you if you want.'

'Yes, please do. Maybe we can build here a small jam factory. There is still so much fruit growing nearby and nobody is buying it. This will be smarter than moving to England. We can even add a special spice and call it 'smart jam'.

'This is a great idea,' said Joanna. 'We can do it.'

As she was saying it, my mother was already in the house, bringing shopping bags into the kitchen. She must have heard what we were talking about as she turned to me and said, 'Making jam? Communist jam?' and then to Joanna, 'did she tell you that she burns everything she cooks and does not even know which bank she keeps her money in? If you want to start a business, better stay away from her. And stop smoking or you'll end up like your mother.'

The Day the Richest Pole Died

The Rs. lived in the last house on our road, in central, yet rural and god-forsaken Poland. One hundred metres north from them was a statue of the Holy Mary, which marked the end of our village. Furthermore there were fields for two or three kilometres, then a railway line and then another village began. During communist times there was always competition between ours and the other village, because the other village had a railway station, while we had a church. When I was a child, the statue marked for me the end of a familiar, safe world. Beyond there were 'the others': people whom I knew nothing of and who felt like a threat. I saw the Rs. as the guardians of our small world and they adopted such a role, informing the neighbours about the developments on the other side. But they were never gossipy or malicious, perhaps because they were the poorest in the neighbourhood and all their energies were invested in surviving the daily hardship.

The old R., whose Christian name I did not know had a small plot of land behind his house, three hectares or so, and worked as a bricklayer in a construction firm in Włocławek, the closest large town. He thus belonged to the category of peasant-workers, who had low status because for the peasants they were not sufficiently rural, and for the workers they were not working class. But most likely he did not care about his status; maybe he was not even fully aware of it. His wife, Franka, as long as I remember, was working the fields; their own plot of land and those of more affluent farmers. She was known for being very good in this work, particularly harvesting potatoes and onions. She was two to three times faster than an average worker, therefore in summer her service was in high demand. The Rs. lived first in a wooden house, which previously belonged to Franka's parents until R. built a small house from a more durable material, which looked like pieces of concrete blocks, used in the 1970s for building high-rise estates. I guess he lifted them from the construction sites on which he was employed. The house seemed to be unfinished, with more windows planned than built, yet was also covered with scars and had aged prematurely, with walls falling apart before they were fully erected. This was despite the fact that the R. (not unlike another builder on our street, the father of my best friend) was spending every weekend on improving his house. After R.'s death the house became surrounded by extensions. They grew like cancer on, by comparison, a healthy body of the main house, being made of poorer materials, with few, very small, windows. For a reason unknown to me the extended parts were dangerously close to the road, although the owners had plenty of space on the other side. Maybe because of having too few windows or to avoid falling into the ditch, the Rs. kept the doors always open, which allowed the passers-by to (over)hear their conversations. Such a habit was acceptable then, when the right to privacy was curtailed by the state, but after the fall of the old system, when people's class position could be easily guessed from the height of their gates and the length of their fences, people like the Rs. started to be seen as a 'problem' waiting to be solved.

By the time R. had finished the first version of his house, the Rs. had one daughter, Maria, and twin sons, Marek and Maciek. R. died when Franka was pregnant with their fourth child, Basia, who was born about fifteen years after their first child. At primary school I was in the same class as Maria. With her dark-blue, velvety eyes and dark hair, common among Mediterranean women, but exceptionally rare in central Poland, she was the prettiest girl in our year. However, she was a very poor pupil. Barely able to read, write and count, she was always on the verge of being sent off to the class for children with learning disabilities. She has repeated some years and finished her education after primary school. Before she reached twenty, she was married to the son of a local peasant, who was also the most unpleasant character in our class. After her wedding Maria disappeared from my radar and indeed she was no longer seen on our road. When I asked Franka what happened to her daughter she replied that she gave birth to a disabled child who was bed-ridden. Consequently, Maria was also, more or less, bed-ridden, taking full responsibility for caring for her offspring. Franka did not hide the fact that Maria's husband mistreated her daughter, accusing her of producing a substandard child. Franka shed a tear when she mentioned it. It was around this time that Franka started to drink, to calm her heart. What she drank she labelled 'little cherry' (wisienka). It was the common name for cheap, fruity wine, regarded by heavier drinkers as extremely unhealthy, although probably much less so than vodka.

Franka's twin sons disappeared from our village soon after they reached adulthood. One joined the army; the other went to work in a coalmine in the South of Poland. The professional soldier fought in Iraq and Afghanistan, got medals for bravery and eventually settled in the South of Poland. He broke ties with his family, apparently on the request of his wife. For his mother, he was a traitor. The miner returned, although initially he did not move back to the village, only brought his daughter, Vanessa, to be looked after temporarily by her grandma, when he was going through a divorce. The girl stayed with the Rs. for two years. As with her aunt, she was an exceptional beauty, with dark eyes, dark hair, large soft lips and glasses which afforded her an intellectual look. She was also gentle, intelligent and discreet. One could talk with her for hours, but do not learn anything about her family or housing situation. Later I noticed that she was friends with the girls from the best houses, without searching for their favours. Eventually Vanessa moved with her father to a nearby town and I stopped seeing her. Franka said that she went to university. Apparently she occasionally visited her grandma and kept in touch with her old friends.

Basia was described by the people in our village as the one who 'did not know her father'. First I took it merely as a statement of the fact, resulting from his premature death. But then I realised there was something more to it: Basia did not know the Freudian 'name of the father': patriarchal authority. Maybe because of that, from an early age she was keen on boys, which inevitably led to gossip. I saw Basia as a transitory figure. In many ways she was a child of Eastern European communism. Although apparently smarter than her older sister, she neglected school and saw no value in education. As with Maria, it never occurred to her that she could do something with her life: get a job or a stall in a market. Unlike her older sister, however, who suffered in silence, she wanted something better from life and acquired some bourgeois habits. She changed the colour of her hair, from super-black to strawberry blond, which did not suit her, painted her toenails and confessed to me that she could not get out of bed without drinking two cups of strong coffee. Basia also did not like to get drunk on 'cherry', preferring vodka mixed with Coca-Cola. Moreover, unlike her mother or sister, Basia did not want just to get married. Her greatest dream was to marry the richest man in Poland. This angered her mother, who used to repeat that all rich men are arseholes: they get rich by taking from the poor.

In our village there was no match for Basia. People there did not have much money and for those better off than the Rs., despite her beauty, Basia had little value, which was further lowered by her being 'easy'. To fulfil her dream, she had to look further afar. The man whom she found turned out to be a short, plump man with coarse features, but he exuded an aura of self-confidence, which some people took for charisma. When he stood at the Rs.' courtyard with his legs spread and arms on his hips, he reminded me of Henry VIII from the famous portrait by Hans Holbein. One could assume that the whole estate was his. Therefore he did not want to work on it; he only requested various changes so that he would not be ashamed to settle there. It did not take Franka much time to figure out that he was a gangster. He turned out to be one of the lowest order. For some years he was robbing provincial shops before being promoted to managing a flock of Romanian prostitutes walking the road near the forest surrounding Włocławek. Whether Basia was aware of that before she tied the knot with him, nobody knew, but most likely it would have made no difference. What counted was that he brought her the luxuries she yearned for: a VHS player, a mobile phone and a car. Well, he did not give her the car, he merely took her for rides and then brought her home. Franka suspected that all these goods were stolen and warned Basia that if their origin was discovered she might get into trouble, but Basia only told her mother to shut up. For her a stolen TV was better than no TV.

Where Basia's husband's permanent address was or even what part of Poland he came from, nobody knew. When asked about his whereabouts, Basia replied that he travelled a lot for business. Later she mentioned that he was building for them a large house near Warsaw, but she was unable to name the suburb where this mansion was to be erected. For the time being, Basia was thus stuck in her old family adobe. Franka alleged that her son in law had a house, but he used it as a training ground for his foreign 'whores'. This situation, in Franka's view, was doubly demeaning for Basia, because she had no access to his house and was below his female employees, who knew more about his life than his family. Franka hated her son in law from the first time she saw him and her loathing grew the more she learnt about him. She never mentioned his name and called him 'This Pimp', 'This Bastard' or 'This Motherfucker', the last name because, as she put it, he was the type who would fuck his own mother if it would bring him profit. She also lost heart for her daughter for being greedy, naïve and a burden to her.

Soon after meeting her future husband, Basia became pregnant and gave birth to a boy, whom she called Bernard. Two years later Brad was born. Such foreign-sounding names, in her mind, testified to her elevated social status. For Franka they only showed that Basia did not know her place. She polonised them, calling one Benek, and the other Bronek. The older boy was like his father: short and plump and with blondish hair, and he adopted the posture of Henry VIII. The younger had Basia's Mediterranean appearance and came across as soft and shy. The older used to call his mother 'You stupid whore'; the younger cuddled to her and cried when his brother insulted her.

The father brought his sons computer games and flashy clothes and took them for rides in his car, in the same way he did earlier with their mother. After performing this ritual he disappeared, to return after weeks or months in increasingly battered vehicles, with some flashy gadgets which, after some time, stopped impressing his sons, as their school mates pointed to their cheapness and obsolescence. The stream of gadgets stopped when he went to prison. Franka hoped that it would put an end to her daughter's ungraceful liaison, but she was proved wrong. Basia remained loyal to her husband and kept visiting him every month or so, as often really as she could afford, given that he lived now over two hundred kilometres from her. She even occasionally engaged in remunerative activity, such as child minding or cleaning, to afford train tickets and presents for her man, so that she did not feel inferior to the wives of other prisoners. Basia got no support from her husband's gangster pals, proving to Franka that not only was he scum, but the lowest sort, commanding no respect even from his own ilk. Franka got so exasperated by the situation that she started to smoke, which, by her own account, burned her lungs and made her weak. Still, despite now being in her seventies, she worked the fields as before because paying for the basics such as food and electricity, was more difficult than ever. As if the situation was not bad enough, during the year of heavy rains their house was flooded. Water destroyed the floors, the meagre furniture and most of the luxuries Basia got from her husband. A neighbour visiting them after this tragedy saw a Nintendo Playstation floating in a pool of dirty water, as if it was a ship. They got no insurance money as their house was, obviously, not insured. Moreover, the flooding revealed that the damaged extensions were built without permission. Franka got a letter asking her to demolish their remains and pay a hefty fine, but it was waived by the local council clerk, proving that people are not heartless or that Polish clerks still enjoy some autonomy. Thanks to the pressure from the neighbours they also got some financial help from the council to repair their house and one neighbour arranged a collection of money and other goods to give to Franka. Normally we would not do it, knowing that she would refuse any help, but this accumulation of misfortune stripped her of some of her pride and she accepted. It also stripped her of her faith in God. 'God died with communism or he is as much of a motherfucker as my son in law,' she said.

After the flooding social services got interested in the welfare of Basia's sons, which added to Franka's stress. Despite loathing her daughter and her son in law, she did not want to lose the boys. Around this time Basia got pregnant again. Her third child was conceived in prison, shortly after the authorities introduced conjugal visits. Nine months after such a visit Basia's youngest son was born. For Franka it was a sign of hope. She loved the boy more than Bernard and Brad because 'he did not know his father.' She herself chose a name for him, Jan, which turned out to be the name of her late husband. However, the new child made things even more difficult than before. Almost every week now Franka and Basia received visits from high-heeled women, who smirked at their poverty and the alleged low standard of hygiene, and warned them that if they did not prove themselves worthy of their children, they would lose them. Franka recounted the visits with the highest indignation. If not for the children, she would have punched these women, who she perceived as getting money from the state which they should have been receiving. Basia was less worried about these visits, having other issues on her mind. These were to do with her husband. While before he kept his family away from his criminal operations, now, being constrained, he wanted her to act as his proxy. What exactly Basia did for him, nobody knew, but her activities upset some people. It was proven one night when two men with their faces covered entered their house and shot Jan. He died on the spot. Why the baby was targeted, rather than Basia or her older sons? The answers to these questions were sought by the neighbours in the months to come. The prevailing hypothesis was that his death had a symbolic value – it was a sign to Basia to stay away from the turf wars in which her husband was engaged.

The murder of Basia's son took place the same day the richest Pole died, in a hospital in Vienna, where he was undergoing some revolutionary treatment, which, however, failed. Judging by its reporting in the news, a saint had passed away. His right to sainthood was ensured by his wealth and his philanthropy. The unspoken assumption of almost everybody publicly commemorating his life, including some high-ranking priests, was that the more wealth, the more charity. For some people in our village the death of the Polish tycoon was, on the other hand, some consolation – a proof that little Jan was somewhat equal to the wealthiest of the world. But others drew attention to their difference: one violent and committed in a household lacking basic amenities; the other in a comfortable and hygienic environment, in a foreign location, underlining the billionaire's cosmopolitan outlook; one happening before conscious life properly started; the other when the man had achieved practically everything there was to achieve and had reached retirement age. For them it was a sign there was no justice in death as there was no justice in life. But the effect of the coincidence of these two deaths was that the demise of the rich man made the neighbours remember the day the boy died. After that whenever anyone asked when little Jan died, the answer was that 'it was the day the richest Pole died.'

In the next three months or so the house of Rs. was emptied. Basia was taken to stand trial for abetting her husband's crimes. Bernard and Brad were sent to foster families. Franka suffered a stroke and was taken to the hospital, where she died without regaining consciousness. The house and the farm were put up for sale and several months later bought by the richest farmer in the neighbouring village. He demolished the Rs' shack and built there a two-storey house for his daughter. Unlike the Rs.' house, which was almost touching the road and revealed its guts to everybody who wanted to look at it, this one was built at a large distance from the road and was best protected of all the houses on our street, with a high fence and three dogs guarding it. Some neighbours showed the house to their visitors saying with bitterness: 'this is our future.'

Disinheritance

In our village there were three families with many children. The Zs. with eleven children were the record-breakers. Then there were the Bs. with eight children and the Ms. with seven. Such large families brought to my mind the stories of prewar times in the Polish countryside, when peasant families were so poor that half of their children died from disease or hunger. Looking at the Zs., the Bs. and the Ms. I wondered how much has changed in rural Poland since then. Did the living conditions improved but people remained the same? It was difficult to say.

The Zs. and the Bs. did not fit the stereotype of a peasant family. Indeed, the Zs. did not fit any recognisable pattern, as from their huge wooden house, strengthened internally with bricks and always undertaking some kind of renovation, originated two teachers, one vice-chairman of the main Polish peasant party, one district scouts' leader, two thieves, one convicted rapist and one mad woman who ended up in a mental asylum (not unlike Mrs. Z., who also lost her mind after so many births). The Bs. did not even have a farm and their children, mostly girls, did quite well in life, becoming teachers and clerks. But the Ms., Roman and Helena, were proper farmers, living from their small plot and services paid to the richer farmers and increasingly non-farmers, so more or less they were like serfs. Other facts pointed to that too. Their large farmhouse felt always dark inside and they lost a large proportion of their offspring before their children reached adulthood. Their oldest son, Kazik, suffered from diabetes, had two legs amputated and died at the age of sixteen. Another son, Bartek, perished in a motorcycle accident, being the passenger of another boy. Their other son also suffered from diabetes and Helena spent a great deal of time travelling with him to a distant town to see specialists.

I used to talk to Roman, who was also my distant cousin from my father's side, when he was coming to cut grass in our garden with his old-fashioned scythe, which was essential to get rid of high grass growing between the trees, or put tar on the roof of the shed. In his peasant way, he was very candid about his personal problems and everything else. Usually he was in good spirits, even when talking about something sad. When I was looking at him, I thought that he must have been handsome in his youth. Even now his muscular body with its natural suntan, his surprisingly dark and thick hair, and relatively delicate hands rendered him almost attractive. My mother said that he was the most attractive of the three sons, in the same way my father was the most attractive of his three siblings, but both were destroyed by their circumstances. Roman's main blemish was his missing teeth; he confessed that fillings and dentures was too much bother for him. When any of his teeth got cavities, he asked the dentist to remove them. And so he was left with maybe ten in total.

When I met Roman the last time, he told me that the death of his sons was not his biggest heartache. Of course, it was a very sad thing, but it was all God's will. Kazik's death even came as a relief as looking after him was a heavy burden for Helena and took a lot of resources which needed to be allocated to their younger children. The greatest problem was that his in-laws had practically disinherited Helena, dividing their land in such a way that most of it went to her older sister and Helena got only a small piece near the wood, where the soil's quality was sub-standard. This decision upset Helena so much that she became sleepless, took up smoking which she had not done for twenty years and stopped seeing a family doctor regarding contraceptives. Because of the disinheritance, she became pregnant again and their last child was born, after a break of almost ten years. Roman was so upset by this new addition to their family that he got drunk as his wife was taken to the hospital. This had not happened with the births of all their other children, as he was not a macho man, enjoying himself when his woman was suffering, and he never liked alcohol, apart from an occasional beer.

'How can parents be so mean to divide their land so unjustly, giving to one child who is better off almost everything and to the other, who is poor, almost nothing?', he asked me, resting on the scythe.

'Did you ask them?' I asked.

'For sure I did,' replied Roman.

'And what did they say?' I asked.

'That they already gave us much money over the years, unlike to Helena's sister and it is not worth giving us more as we are like a sieve, without a bottom. We spend everything on our children rather than modernising our farm. They don't see us as humans, but as some pest which proliferates when it gets more nourishment.'

'What would the priest say to that?' I asked, not out of curiosity, but embarrassment, as I did not know what else to say.

'I do not talk to priests. Like everybody, they look down on people with many children. They regard them as stupid, not good Catholics. And probably rightly so.'

'The Wałęsas also have many children,' I remarked, again, just to say something.

'Well, yes. And therefore Wałęsa is seen as stupid and his children are the laughing stock of the whole country'.

We were about to finish this talk, when Roman added, 'This is not the first time we were disinherited. Previously my father hurt me when he gave the good land to Ryszard and to me what was practically fallow land. When I realised what happened, I felt like killing him, but by this point my father was already dead.'

'Why did it happen?'

'Ryszard was always sly and manipulated my father. And the irony is that he even did not need the land as he is not a farmer, but some kind of property developer. And he is doing well in Lublin, the motherfucker.'

Then he pointed to our house and land and asked: 'What about you? What you and Magda will do with it when your mother dies?'

'Magda wants to sell her part. I will probably keep mine.'

'This is the right thing to do. One shouldn't sell the land. One should always pass it to one's children.'

'Our farm is of no use to my children. They are not even Polish anymore.'

'You are Polish, so they are Polish too. And they might need the farm one day. There might be war and hunger in the city and then a cow and some chicken will be of use.'

'They will not travel from England to rear chicken here. They don't even eat meat'.

There was no point to prolong the discussion. I left and Roman finished cutting the grass.

I haven't heard about Roman for almost a year, till in my weekly telephone conversation with my mother she told me that he went to prison for assaulting his brother with an axe. The story was that his brother, Ryszard, the one who moved to a different part of Poland and got rich there offered to swap Roman's fallow land for a piece of land of much higher quality. Ryszard presented it as a way to make up for the harm inflicted on Roman by their parents. Roman agreed and the appropriate act was signed with the notary, only to learn later that the value of this land which he swapped was many times higher than his brother's, due to the fact that a motorway was meant to be built in its proximity. Thus Roman's own brother effectively cheated him. This made Roman so angry that he went to his home with the axe. He did not kill him, either because the brother disarmed him or he changed his mind, but the police were called and took Roman away. Apparently this event upset Helena so much that she tried to take her own life, hanging herself in a barn, but she nailed the hook to a rotten plank in the ceiling which detached itself at the crucial moment. All in all, as my mother said, this was worse than the Holocaust. Plus now, with Roman in jail, there was nobody in our village to cut our grass with a scythe; so my mother had to use scissors to get rid of the grass around the trees.

'There was collection for money for Helena and the children. I paid for all three of us', said my mother. 'The people decided that we will do so every month. Are you OK with?'

'Yes, this is fine.'

That evening I watched 'Taxidermia,' a grim Hungarian film about three generations of Hungarians, who live and die in an undignified way, with the youngest, the taxidermist, cutting himself into half using complicated machinery, to become an object of art, displayed in an art gallery. It occurred to me that such a film could not be set in Poland, where ropes, axes and naked hands are still the principal ways of finishing life prematurely. I found this thought comforting – if I was to be murdered, better to be killed with an axe, than be tortured beforehand and displayed later. Better to die the serfs' than the artist's death.

The Widow and Her Daughter

Of all the houses on our street, the last but one was the most mysterious to me. Or, to be precise, first it was simply unknown; there was no mystery, because there was no curiosity on my part to learn what was going on there. I knew that the people who lived there were an old widow and her daughter. The widow was not unfriendly, but she wasn't one for small talk or gossip. As for her daughter, apparently she was a good pupil, but quiet and not one of the teacher's favourites. For Christmas and Easter the widow and her daughter stayed in their home and nobody visited them. One could see them in the church, sitting some distance from the altar, as if not to attract attention, although nobody paid much attention to them anyway. The only person in my family who had any relation with the widow was my granny, who exchanged seeds and plants with her. She claimed that the widow had the best cucumbers and tomatoes on our street and she was the first to try new vegetables such as peppers and oddly shaped pumpkins, whose proper name 'squash' I learnt many years later. At some stage the daughter left our village to study biology or chemistry in Toruń, but she returned home after finishing her education, and became a teacher in a neighbouring village. Some years later she was promoted to headmistress in the same school. She was the first female teacher in our village to drive her own car, although nobody saw her having driving lessons, passing a test or taking advice where to get the best bargain for the car. People assumed that the money for the car came from renting their land. The car added to the daughter's unknowability, as one cannot see car drivers properly, in contrast to cyclists who cannot easily ignore those shouting at them.

By the time I asked my mother what happened to these distant neighbours, the daughter was in her forties and she was still unmarried and lived with her mother. This was an uncommon position for women in our village, except that it befell female teachers more often than members of any other occupational groups, simply because teachers in Poland are mostly women, so they have few opportunities for office ro-mance and live under pressure to behave modestly. To that I shall add that the widow's daughter wasn't a beauty. She had a square peasant face, bluntly cut mousy blonde hair which looked greasy even when freshly washed and a stocky body, clad in timeless shapeless brown or grey skirts or trousers of the same colour. But she wasn't ugly either; just plain. Our village was full of people who looked like her and it wasn't difficult to imagine her going to the altar with her male equivalent.

One thing which made the house where the widow and her daughter lived unknowable was that it was built kind of back to front. The front facing the street had only two narrow windows, like squinted spying eyes, turned 180 degrees. By contrast, the back of the house had two large windows and wide double doors, overseeing a large backyard. When my granny used to visit the widow and the widow was in charge of the house, it was an ordinary backyard with hens pecking at the grass. The garden with these magnificent vegetables was then at the front of the house. It was not surrounded by a fence, but by tall hollyhocks, always gently moving in the wind and proudly displaying their flowers, like some exotic naked women showing their breasts in a ceremonial dance.

When the daughter returned to live back with her mother, she took over the estate and things started to change. She got rid of the hollyhocks and erected a tall fence. Where there used to be a vegetable garden, there was now a flower garden and the vegetable garden was reduced and moved to a distant corner, on the right side of the house It stopped looking like a proper vegetable garden and more like an inroad into the field of their neighbour, who grew potatoes and fodder beets.

The real change happened at the courtyard. The hens disappeared and the large space was transformed into an exotic flower display, with the plants showcased in fancy pots and arranged on special ladders or other contraptions. They flowered even in winter, thanks to the daughter moving them to a fancy greenhouse. Such a conspicuous display was completely untypical of our village, where people grew flowers, but didn't arrange them. What was even more unusual was that this exotic collection was private – the flowers couldn't be seen from the street. To see them, people had to enter the courtyard. This required knocking and pretending that they had an errand for the widow or her daughter. Most of the time, however, nobody let them in.

People gossiped that the widow was there, but the daughter locked her up and didn't allow her to have any guests. I, for that matter, hadn't seen the widow for ages, but once, when I passed by their house cycling, I spotted her extracting the weeds from the vegetable garden. She saw me too and waved to me, so I stopped my bike and walked through the field to meet her. I was surprised that she recognised me, given that we never had a proper conversation, at least not since the death of my granny.

'You are Mrs. K's granddaughter, aren't you?' she asked me rhetorically, yet, straight to the point.

'I am.'

'But you don't live here anymore?' she asked.

'Indeed, I moved away many years ago, but keep coming back every summer.'

'When your granny was alive, we had the best gardens on our street and even in the whole village. Her parsnips were huge, tasty and stayed fresh the whole year. Her spice plantation was also unbeatable and she gave everybody dill and horseradish for making sour cucumbers. But I had the best tomatoes and beans, because at the time I was able to travel to Włocławek or even Bydgoszcz to buy new seeds and plants. Now, I couldn't go to Włocławek– too much hassle and my daughter wouldn't allow me. She says I'm senile and need to stay at home, because otherwise I will be lost.'

I replied, to be polite: 'Your daughter must had inherited your green hands, given the flower display in the backyard.'

'Well, she doesn't plant or prune them. She just buys them and sticks them on these contraptions. For me, they are dead.'

'But they are beautiful,' I said. 'I've never seen anything like that anywhere else in Poland.'

'Well, she travels far away to get them, sometimes as far as Białystok or Wrocław. The girl only has two things on her mind: flowers and the church.'

'I didn't know she was so religious.'

'Yes, she was and it's got worse since she retired. She goes on these various religious pilgrimages and gatherings. Often she goes to the flower market and religious events at the same time, going away for three or four days at a time.'

But there was no pride in the widow's voice, only sadness. 'You know, she's a spinster, this daughter of mine.'

'Yes, I know.'

'She likes it this way. Even when she was a teenager, she said that she would't get married because she couldn't allow a nasty or ugly man enter our house.'

'She must have been a strong character then, your daughter,' I said.

'Yes, she is,' the widow admitted.

I couldn't stay much longer, so I left and didn't hear about the widow and her daughter for a long time – till the daughter died. Her death was remarkable and shed new light on her passion for collecting beautiful flowers. It turned out that she had a heart attack when attending a peep show in the East of Poland, looking at young male strippers from Ukraine, performing for private clients. She was sixty-five. Such performances were the real goals of her 'religious pilgrimages.' I couldn't help but smile when a neighbour told me, realising that in our village we have our own versions of the main literary types, including a female version of Professor Aschenbach from Thomas Mann's novella, dying in the moment of a voyeuristic ecstasy.

'Does the widow know what killed her daughter?'

'No,' the neighbour said. 'We decided that it was better to keep her in the dark. She thinks she died at some religious meeting. Which is true, in a sense,' giggled the neighbour.

'What will happen to the widow?' I asked.

'She will go to the old people's home, I guess,' said the neighbour. 'She has nobody to look after her, but she has money, plenty of money, especially if she sells the house and the land. It is worth hundreds of thousands of Euros these days.'

'It makes sense to sell it,' I said, although it caused me sorrow to think about all the houses and farms in our village which were passing to strangers.

Then I stopped thinking about the widow, again, assuming that she died. But then, several years after learning about the fate of her daughter, when cycling, I spotted her in her garden. This time she didn't wave to me, but I decided to approach her of my own accord. She was using a walking stick now and a special weeding tool which didn't require for her to kneel down. She was also wearing a hearing aid, which was a relief, as it meant that I didn't need to shout to her.

Again, she recognised me and told me, showing me her weeding tool: 'This was made especially for me. It has different endings for different actions. I paid two thousand zloty for it, but it's worth every penny. Still, I cannot do everything in the garden or at home myself. A gardener comes once a week to help me and a nurse every day.'

'It's great that you can still live in your own home,' I said.

'Yes, it is. One doctor wanted to send me to a nursing home, but I objected. A special committee from Bydgoszcz came to assess me and agreed that I was okay to be on my own and, besides, there were no places in any nursing home this side of Włoclawek.'

'This is great,' I repeated, 'but a shame there are no places for old folk.'

'Do you know how old I am?' she asked me.

'I don't know,' I replied.

'One hundred and one. Most people think that I should have died a long time ago, given that my life has been so bare - I lost my husband early, my sister died in her sixties, I had no grandchildren and now my only daughter is dead. Truth be told, I'm not afraid to die, but I still enjoy living. My garden keeps me going.'

I realised that it was also what my granny used to say. I didn't begrudge the widow her longevity, but I was sad thinking that our garden hadn't kept my granny as long as the widow.

It was the late August and the widow's garden was full of vegetables. She gave me a plastic bag in which I put some cucumbers, tomatoes and beans.

'Take as much as you want as in two days the rest will be collected by Mr. M' (who was another neighbour). And when I was leaving, she told me:

'You look like your granny. She also had these light-blue eyes and a crooked her head like that when she was talking', she said. 'I do miss her badly,' she said.

'So do I,' I replied and mounted my bike.

Summer After Summer

Krystyna was in the same primary school as me, but one year below me, therefore we never had a chance to know each other well. But she fascinated me with her almost oriental beauty – very dark hair, dark eyes and lashes, thick eyebrows, dark complexion, and graceful movements of her tall and slender body. The only flaw was a scar on her cheek, a memory of some childhood accident or illness. I admired not only her beauty, but this scar. For me it was a sign the fate wanted to prevent her from being too attractive, which only proved that she was unusually beautiful. I also admired the fact that she behaved as if she was unaware of her attractiveness. She wore her hair in a simple ponytail and on school photos she always stood on the far side, at the back, allowing other girls to take centre stage.

As I went to secondary school in a different town and gradually moved further and further from my village I would see Krystyna only occasionally, typically in summer. During my visits I learnt that she became a midwife and married Tomek, a boy from her class in primary school. Tomek was the youngest of three brothers and one could see that the older ones sucked all the attractiveness and acumen allocated to this family by the Almighty. They were tall and good-looking with dark hair and expressive eyes, while Tomek was short, with narrow eyes, wide lips and blondish hair, which stubbornly refused to be tamed by a comb. Both of Tomek's brothers got managerial positions in large factories in Włocławek, and when these factories got privatised, they acquired a large chunk of their shares and set up their own lucrative businesses. Tomek moved from one dead-end job to another and eventually ended up working for one of his brothers. One might wonder why Krystyna chose such an unattractive loser, but a large part of the answer was that there weren't many men to choose from in our village: any non-drunkard and non-wife-beater was regarded as good material for a husband. According to the gossip, Tomek was also very persistent in his courtship, ensnaring Krystyna like Soames Forsyte Irene from *The Forsyte Saga*, the series we all watched as teenagers.

It was a long time until Krystyna and I had a proper conversation and this happened when my mother was looking for a companion for Andrew, preferably a boy his age, when I was to go away for almost two weeks, leaving her to look after her grandson by herself. In summer finding such a companion was difficult, as most kids were on vacations and those who didn't go, according to my mother, were too rough to be allowed into our house. When she exhausted all the possibilities, it occurred to her that Maciek, Krystyna's son, would do. He was twelve or thirteen, five or six years older than Andrew, but he had Down syndrome, so intellectually they'd probably suit each other. My mother first approached Maciek's grandmother, with whom she was friends, and then we walked to Krystyna's house with Andrew, to introduce the boys to each other and see how they got along. The house was a hybrid between an old-style box-shaped house, typical for the 1970s and 1980s, when people were hungry for living space and the postcommunist nouveau riche residence, in which style was as important as size. It was grey and angular, but had a slightly sloping roof, a porch and a well-groomed garden. The estate on which it was built came into existence in the last years of the 'communist' rule and was full by the early 1990s. Most houses there looked similar to that belonging to Krystyna and Tomek; they reflected the hopes of the new system, which weren't quite fulfilled. Many simultaneously concealed and revealed stories of unemployment and bankruptcies, through their neglected façades, very old German cars in the driveways and on occasion, 'For Sale' signs.

When we were introduced to Maciek, I noticed that he looked like his father in his youth, except that he had a slightly shorter neck and flatter face, and was stouter than him – a result of over-supply of sweeties by one of his grandmas. Maciek's older sister, Dorota, was also physically similar to her father. This similarity seemed to be a source of her discomfort. When she stood next to her stunning mother, she would touch her hair nervously or cover her mouth, as if trying to hide the things which made her so different from her. All in all, it felt as if Tomek's genes were adamant to overpower any other genes.

Maciek and Andrew's first meeting indicated that the boys would get on fine. They both liked watching cartoons and were fans of the 'Ben 10' series, as proved by a large collection of 'Ben 10' toys, meticulously arranged on the shelves. The speech of our sons was also slightly impaired, albeit for different reason, which paradoxically helped their communication, as they didn't mind not understanding everything.

I suggested that one day Andrew could visit Maciek and the next Maciek could come to our house, but Krystyna said that it wasn't a good idea, as Maciek wasn't used to leaving his comfort zone. Luckily Andrew didn't mind to be half a day away from home. He was happy to have a new friend, access to a big supply of toys and a large television.

When I returned from my trip, Krystyna suggested that the boys continue to play together. This time it was my turn to supervise them. I tried to take them outdoors, to cycle or play ball. Maciek had a tricycle, but he wanted to try my bike and a after couple of minutes of quivering and wobbling, started to cycle properly and so fast that Andrew struggled to keep up. It was also during our time together that I noticed that he was very perceptive and in a simple way was able to provide an accurate portrait of his family, using just one word to describe each member. One of his grandmas was 'soft'; the other was 'loud'; his sister was 'quiet'; his mother was 'kind' and he was 'good'. The only person for whom he had no adjectives was his father, who was 'there' – locked in his room. Indeed, apart from his genes, Tomek was noticeable most by his absence, which was equally accented. The space around his study-cum-workshop was ominously curved; nobody seemed to have the courage to disturb him or even risk coming too close to him. On the subsequent visits, the only time when I saw Tomek leaving his room, was to complain about the noise.

Before Andrew and I returned to England, Krystyna and I went to the café in the park - the only café in our village, only open in summer and only at the weekends. From our table we could observe people going to church or the supermarket, and some children playing on seesaws in another corner of the park.

'Do you remember that when we were children, this park was full of drunkards and retards?', asked Krystyna.

'Yes, I do. I still remember a woman who spat and shouted obscenities at passers-by and another with a large red bow in her hair.'

'The first was called Nanny Goat, because of her swearing. She was impossible to stop. The second was quieter. She became popular among the boys who were too shy to lose their virginity with normal girls. There were many others too, because behind the corner there was a special school. Almost every teacher from our primary school wanted to move there, because there was less work and salaries were higher. My mother got very bitter, because for many years she couldn't get in; she was outflanked by other teachers; as a PE teacher she was the last in line. It was only two years before her retirement that she moved there, but now she has a "special child" to teach for the rest of her life,' said Krystyna and after a while she continued with a nostalgic smile:

'The retards used to come here during breaks and after school. After 3 p.m. there were at least ten of them at any given time and in the summer they would hold their own parties with lemonade and cheap wine.'

'What happened to them?' I asked.

'The older ones died, the younger ones got moved on and the next generation got aborted. The special school was closed down even before Maciek was born due to the lack of children and funds. The language got more polite; now people don't use words like "retards" and "freaks", only "people with mental disabilities", but the attitudes to them got harsher. Nobody wants to see them on the streets or in school. They say this is because they don't want the unfortunate to be bullied, but the truth is that they don't want them to spoil their pristine neighbourhood.'

The occasion required an expression of deep concern, but instead I giggled, thinking about the village idiots. It seemed that Krystyna didn't notice, as she continued:

'You wonder why Maciek was born. This was Tomek's idea. Not that he was anti-abortionist as such, but he wanted us to make a sacrifice. Even when we were in secondary school, he was the only one in the class who read Polish romantic literature as if this was something about his own life. He wanted to be like the nineteenth century insurrectionist who gave his life for the freedom of his country. Back then it charmed me. It was only some years later that I noticed that he preferred to dream about noble deeds behind closed doors, yet expected me to go out and make them happen. The more he was outpaced by others in real life, the loftier became his ideas and the more pompous a loser he became'.

'So you regret that Maciek was born?' I asked,.

'I do. Not because he is a burden, but because he is lonely. He only knows his family. I don't know what will happen to him when we die. I just pray he dies before us.'

As I wasn't good at changing the subject, Krystyna petered off and we sat in silence. . The waiter came, asking us if we wanted to order something else. We didn't, so we left, passing the old 'special school', which had become an economics and management college. Apparently the school struggled to re- cruit, despite offering courses in 'agrotourism management' and 'PR in agriculture'. According to my mother, it was pre- cisely because of these fake titles that the local farmers didn't want to send their children there.

The next summer I kept bringing Andrew to Krystyna's house and the boys played together, although Andrew did so reluctantly because by this point he preferred cycling with me to the lake and his 'Ben Ten' stage had passed. Moreover, he didn't like when Tomek was at home, as it meant that the television had to be turned down and there was a bad atmosphere in the house.

One year later Andrew didn't want to visit Maciek at all, because he was even more keen to spend his days cycling and he befriended a group of local boys roughly his age, with whom he went to the local park or the pizza parlour. Once or twice I suggested that they take Maciek with them, but he refused, saying that Maciek wouldn't fit in and the other boys wouldn't like it. This summer I didn't visit Krystyna either, as I was too embarrassed to tell her that Andrew exchanged his old friend for a new company, even though she wouldn't begrudge my son for that.

Another year passed and most likely I would not see more of Krystyna, except for the brief moments when our bikes passed each other on the way to the grocery shop, if not for the fact that I had learnt that Tomek drowned on a holiday at the Baltic coast, when trying to rescue a drowning teenager. I decided to visit her, not so much to offer her my condolences, as to find out how she was coping. As I expected, Krystyna wasn't grieving. For one, she couldn't afford it. There were the usual bills to pay and some extra expenses, related to Dorota's studies and Maciek's health. He started to suffer from breathing problems and she was taking him to a specialist in a different part of the country. She'd decided to give up her work at the hospital as it was too poorly paid and had set up her own business, assisting home births. For that, she'd started learning to drive.

There were so many news that we almost forgot to talk about the accident at the seaside. It turned out that Tomek managed to bring the boy to safety, but once on the beach, Tomek's heart stopped working and he died within minutes.

'He had a weak heart, which he used as an excuse not to do much around the house and to lock himself in his room so he could imagine himself as some Polish general assisting Napoleon or liberating Hungary. But I never believed that he would actually try to do anything heroic. Maybe I didn't know him that well. Anyway, he must have been happy to have this guy clinging to him, as it was as close to fighting in the uprising as he could get in this time of peace. And equally in vain,' she added with a sad smile.

'He rescued somebody,' I said. 'So maybe it wasn't in vain.'

'Well, it transpired that the boy was a junkie and he died several months later from an overdose. I keep quiet about it, so that the neighbours don't think of us as even bigger losers than we already are.'

Krystyna said this with the same impassive voice which she always used. Her inability to show outrage impressed me most about her, even though I knew that it was a protective device.

Before I left, I spent some time talking to Maciek. Since my previous visit he lost quite a lot of weight. This was because Krystyna was adamant that he didn't get obese as it would make his breathing problem worse. He also started to learn English; every week a teacher came to his home. Yet, the death of his father didn't change much in his general outlook. He was still 'good', his mother was 'kind', his grandmother was 'loud' and the father was still 'there'; except that the position of his hand changed as he said it, with his fingers pointing slightly higher than before, as if Tomek was now occupying the space between heaven and his old study.

A couple of summers passed and I decided to visit Krystyna again. I came on a Sunday afternoon without announcing myself and it turned out that she had a guest – a handsome tall man with dark hair in his forties. When I arrived, they were drinking coffee in the sitting room. Inevitably, I felt like an intruder and wanted to leave, but Krystyna insisted I stay. I was informed that the visitor was living in Szczecin and had his own IT business. I gathered that he was well off, as proved by his perfect haircut and discretely elegant clothes, as well as a new Audi parked in the driveway. When we finished our coffee, Krystyna asked me if I wanted to see Maciek and we went to his room, where he was playing with a girl named Kasia, who also had Down syndrome. It turned out that she was three years younger than Maciek, but came across as more boisterous than him. Unlike Maciek, she went to school and had private lessons in English, Spanish and was learning piano. I looked around and noticed that he still had 'Ben 10' on his shelves, but they moved into the background, becoming a memory of his childhood. New things filled his room – an iPad, a laptop, a smartphone and these were the objects Maciek played with Kasia. He was better with technology than her and was happy to show her his skills.

Krystyna asked me if I would like to come another day, but I said that I wouldn't have time this summer, as I had to visit relatives in different parts in Poland before returning to Britain. However, the real reason was that I wanted to keep the image of the happy family intact, at least till the next summer.

The House with a Mezzanine

When I was a child, Iza was my best friend. We lived on the same street, in small houses without facilities, as was the case in Poland at the time, in the 1970s. The difference was that we had a farm, an orchard and plenty of farm buildings where one could hide and play, while there was not much space around Iza's house. The lack of space was do with the fact that her father, who was a builder, kept extending the house with verandas, balconies and other such additions, which ate into the already small garden and courtyard. He also made sure that the whole property was as saturated in concrete as possible. Concrete was his personal signature. He played with this material in the same way children play with plasticine. Even his way to render their garden unique was to erect a miniature concrete chapel dedicated to the Holy Mary, decorated with plastic flowers. Trees were of little importance to him, so he never pruned them, unlike most of his neighbours, but despite that, they had the best plums in the neighbourhood and their branches bent on the street, inviting the passers-by to pick the fruit.

Inside the house walls were always in transition. Floors went up, ceilings went down or vice versa, to allow for an extra room, to extend a ceiling or divide a pantry into two areas. Needless to say, the house did not look particularly well-proportioned and made his wife and daughters restless. But they could not do much about it, as he was a tyrant, and Iza's mother took pride in enduring her husband's building excesses. I called Iza's abode 'the house with the mezzanine', borrowing this title from Chekvov, partly on the account of the shape of her house and partly because she reminded me of Leda, one the characters of the story. Iza was not as stern as Chekhov's Leda, but like her, she was filled with a sense of rightness. She was a natural social conservative; she condemned homosexuality, prostitution, and letting children to play unsupervised. Looking back, I cannot understand how we survived as friends, given that I could not stand such behaviour. The answer might lie simply in the physical proximity of our houses; we had nobody else to play with on our street.

True to her vocation, Iza became a teacher, and later a headmistress in a large school in a different part of Poland, still in a province, but more affluent than our region. Since her promotion she acquired various habits, which reflected her new bourgeois status, but also confirmed her provinciality. She no longer went out of the house in slippers or with wet hair, and what we called Sunday clothes became her daily attire. She stopped visiting neighbours without telephoning them first, and she got herself a car, which she used even for short distances. Asked why she did not use a bike, she replied that she forgot how to cycle. No wonder, she gained weight and even looked older than her real age. Her matronly look fitted her views, which she presented in a solemn way, indicating that under no circumstances would she change them.

Because we both lived far away from our family homes, our contact became less regular. Still, we tended to see each other every summer, when we visited our families. Usually Iza came to our house as she did not like me to visiting her. When her father was still alive, I was thinking that this was because of her father, who in old age started to talk nonsense. But even after the death of her parents, she did not like me to go there. At the time I was not sure why, but didn't dare to ask her. I told myself that maybe she did not like the atmosphere of the empty house. At this stage, she started to call it her 'summer retreat', suggesting that she went there in the same way the townies go on holiday, although for us it was not going away, but coming home. Since the death of her mother the main reason to return were her visits to the church and the graveyard. She paid handsome money for church services for her parents and in summer she used to leave for church as early as half past five in the morning, to make sure that the priest did not squander her money, which she expected him to do when she was not checking up on him.

For many years Iza tended to visit our village with her husband, who stayed there for the whole duration of their holiday. Later his visits got shorter and then he stopped coming. We learnt that he lost his job, but the rumour was that he survived financially thanks to playing the stock market and engaging in some shadowy businesses. Eventually he left Iza for a younger woman who lived in the same tenement block. The year it happened Iza did not come to our village in the summer and the next year I was there so little that I missed her. When we met up again, it was already over two years after her divorce. On this occasion she invited me to her house, most likely because she did not want my mother to listen to our conversation. As I expected, she wanted to talk about her ex-husband misdemeanours, going through them with a precision of an accountant. She mentioned that he was poor with money, unreliable, he easily got into conflicts with people, he had a younger brother who was even worse than him, and he had diabetes and was infertile. He was not good from the start and things only went worse with time.

I showed Iza sympathy, but then told her: 'Almost every woman on our street wanted her husband to die, including our mothers. And you managed to get rid of him before he died. Shouldn't you be happy about it?'

'No. All my life was about putting up with him, like my mother was putting up with my father. Now there is nobody to pay me for my suffering. And he is lucky twice, even though this woman is obviously a whore, and a stupid one, for that.'

There was no point to tell her to find another man. For women in our village men were like purgatory, which for the lucky ones might lead to a heaven of widowhood. Only an idiot would like to go through purgatory twice.

'Who knows? Maybe this woman will make him pay for your suffering. This often happens in life.'

'This never happens to me. People always harm me and get away with it. You too', said Iza.

'What do you mean?', I asked.

'Do you remember the copybook with silver and golden paper for making cutaways? You once gave it to me and then changed your mind and wanted to get it back and you sent your grandma to take it back. She told my mother that I stole it from you. So my mum spanked me for thieving.'

'I don't remember it. Anyway, it must had happened forty years ago, if not more.'

'But I remember it well: the shame, the humiliation. And you never apologised. You always did what you wanted and your grandma defended you no matter what, so you grew up moody, spoilt and condescending. You didn't even need to say anything. It was enough that you came to our house and looked at it in your patronising way, like a princess visiting the servants' quarters. You were always so selfish and insensitive, yet you always had such an easy life.'

'I wouldn't say my life was so easy', I said. 'But never mind.'

I tried to change the subject as the atmosphere was heavy, but it took me a while to find a new subject. Eventually I asked: 'What will you do with the house?'

'I will sell it. I never liked it. These small rooms and silly extensions are embarrassing and there might be even asbestos in these walls. I always wanted to have a house with large rooms, a proper garden and grass around the house, as you had. Maybe I will buy the house of Szs., as it is also on sale.'

'What you do if nobody will buy it?'

'I will burn it. I cannot live with this monstrosity.'

I did not find the house monstrous. On the contrary, on this occasion I liked it as never before. With the small rooms and low ceilings and filing cabinets full of crystal glasses and decorated plates, it felt like a doll's house. Only now I realised that Iza's father's grand ambition was to build a simulacra of a manor house. Probably Mr. B. got the idea from watching Polish television series where one could see frequently such houses. This was reflected in the appearance of the house front and the style of the furniture and pictures hanging on the walls – he was trying to buy 'vintage' stuff before it was fashionable. Just the house's smallness and the fact that it was always under construction obscured this fact.

I planned to pick up some plums from Iza's plum's tree which, despite being very old, still produced plenty of fruit, but after learning about the debt of silver paper lost my courage to do it. Back at home I told my mother about Iza's plans to swap her house for that of the Szs., and she was very disapproving, as she disliked when people from our village did not know their place, metaphorically or literally.

It turned out that Iza's plan could not materialise, because the potential buyers of her house did not have enough cash and could not get a mortgage due to its ceiling being several centimetres too low to satisfy some health and safety requirements the bank required. Iza was thus stuck with it for time being. I thought it would add to her sense of injustice and made her even more bitter, but when I met her two years later, she was much more content with her life. Her ex-husband got stroke and was now semi-paralysed and Iza discovered the pleasures of travelling. She even mentioned that in-between visiting Barcelona, Paris and Milan it was nice to visit the house with the mezzanine to chill out. Even the plums tasted better after comparing them with the fruit elsewhere. She planned to plant new plum trees in autumn.

The Hunter of Negativity

When I left the supermarket on Christmas Eve, I noticed that my bike fell over. I picked it up and tried to ride, but it did not want to go. The wheels behaved as if they were locked. It was really annoying as I had two large bags full of shopping and the supermarket was at the very end of my village. There was nobody to ask for help. But then somebody said: 'These shitty Polish bikes. They bend all over when the smallest wind blows.'

I did not need to look up to know who said these words. It was my second cousin Ryszard. Without asking me, he put the bike upside down and started to kick its wheels and press its spokes. When he finished the job, he said, 'Hopeless junk, unlike the old Russian ones which one could throw from the Palace of Culture and find them unscathed on the pavement. Still, you should be able to reach home on it' and then added, 'You shouldn't leave a bike like that. Couldn't you see that there are here these special stands for bikes? They're there to be used.'

'I know, but I don't like them. Thanks a lot and Merry Christmas,',I said, to which he replied:

'For you it might be merry. You have nothing to complain about. But for me,' – he did not finish the sentence, just made a sign with his hand, pointing his thumb down. It was, however, not the usual sign of defeat, but defeat multiplied, with his hand lowered down so it almost touched the pavement, pointing to a hole in the ground – a road to hell he knew well.

'Don't fall there,' he said as I was mounting my bike.

'Okay, thanks. I have to rush home,' I said, suddenly worried that he might invite himself to my mother's house. He must have read my thoughts, as he added:

'And tell your mother that I will not visit her today or tomorrow, or any other day, for that matter. Tell her that I don't want to have anything to do with her anymore.'

'OK. Merry Christmas and Happy New Year!' I said, jumping on my bike and feeling the familiar unease inside.

It was obvious to me that I would not tell my mother what my cousin said, but it would be difficult to withhold it from Andrew. Although Andrew avoided Ryszard, he did not mind talking about him, not in a gossipy way, but to learn something about – for the lack of a better world – I will call 'human nature'. It was indeed Andrew who started to 'theorise' Ryszard by placing him in the broad category of 'local creeps'. This category included people from my past, whom we did not like to meet. One such person was the Creep in Red Shoes. I did not know his name, but he knew mine and always shouted at me when we passed through the village on our bikes. Once or twice he also joined us when Andrew was eating ice cream sitting on a bench in the market square, asking how things were going in my life. The question by itself was innocuous, but the sense of intimacy the Creep projected and the creepiness of his entire demeanour, marked by his red sports shoes, with shoe laces nonchalantly undone, jeans torn at his knees and coupled with a fake army jacket, all so unsuitable to the unselfconscious provinciality of my village and his age (he must have been in his early fifties when he adopted such look), was very creepy and made Andrew cringe. Another case was the Weirdo Who Was in Love with

Me. Apparently, I rejected his advances forty years previously, humiliating him deeply, therefore in his opinion I owed him at least a kiss on his mouth. Then there was the Slimy Drunkard who used to address all older women with spare cash with titles such as 'Mrs. Manageress' or 'Mrs Chairwoman' or even 'Your Highness', grabbing their hands to place on them his slimy kiss in exchange for a small financial support. This guy was eventually found dead under an oak tree in the park hugging am empty bottle of vodka, with saliva frozen into a small icicle.

These were the 'straight creeps'. Ryszard wasn't creepy in this way, or at least this ordinary lack of attractiveness accounted for a small percentage of his overall creepiness. He was off-putting due to his personality, not the way he looked. Andrew summarised it by giving him the name the Hunter of Negativity. This was because he had an immense capacity for finding flaws in everything: people, institutions, social structures, life itself. Admittedly, it's not such a difficult task, given that life is not a bed of roses. Yet, I did not know anybody who applied himself to such a task with comparative zeal and thoroughness. To extract maximum negativity from the flow of human life, Ryszard mentally divided it into different layers, requiring different care.

The most superficial concerned the ordinary misfortune. Having plenty of time, he used it to listen to what the village people had to say, trying to extract from their stories the negative core. It wasn't too difficult, as people in our village, as everywhere, were divorcing, dying from cancer and on occasion even committing suicide and killing each other. He collected them and disseminated them, usually adding one or two gruesome details. For example, when one of our neighbours died by hanging himself, he added that his dying was prolonged by the board in the ceiling, to which he attached the rope, being rotten, it left him hanging for hours with one leg practically touching the ground.

Ryszard made the most of such incidents, as every bad occurrence counted, but they did not excite him, being too straightforward. The more attractive were the seemingly happy events, because they contained in them a seed of tragedy. Weddings meant the beginning of a poison and hatred, the birth of a child meant that one would be screwed up by an ungrateful parasite for decades. He followed these routes, creating mental charts for everybody whom people in the village regarded as successful, waiting patiently for their downfall. And if there was no obvious downfall, he conjured one up – claiming that he knew something about these people the rest of the village did not know: extra-marital affairs, bribery, drugs. In his perception tragedies always befell men; women were merely their instruments and their misery did not have any autonomous value. Another layer of life, from which Ryszard extracted negativity, was existential. He revelled in the passage of years which robbed people of their health and beauty. For example, once or twice, when we were sitting at the shore of the lake, he touched my naked thigh to show me the spots or sagging flesh, saying, 'It doesn't look good, does it? Still, somebody might agree to shag you,' adding after a while with a laugh, 'if you pay them.'

Such talk, fuelled by his misogyny and spite, upset Andrew, but there was no point in trying to put Ryszard off from peddling his obscenities. His answer would be that he acts in good faith, vaccinating my son against dirtier talk – as life is dirty and cruel. So, we tried to avoid Ryszard. However, avoiding him was more difficult than the other local creeps and weirdos, because he was a family member and he sought our company. He requested my mother to inform him what we were doing and made an effort to identify patterns in our activities, so that he could stalk us, if we did not give into his company voluntarily. Over the years, we learnt how to avoid him, but he was always one step ahead of us, appearing when we least expected him, piercing me with his gaze, in which accusation and triumph mixed in equal proportions.

Ryszard stalked me not just out of desire to upset me but also from the conviction that we had much in common. First, we were family – the same blood flew through our veins. Ryszard's father was a prisoner of Auschwitz and Gusen, as was my grandfather. For me this shared past was practically meaningless, as I felt no trauma related to the death of those ancestors whom I never met, but Ryszard claimed that we were both sufferers, no matter whether I felt this way or not. He, of course, suffered more, despite the fact that his father survived the camps, while my grandfather died in Gusen. The fact that our ancestors ended up in Austria also meant that they knew other countries and cultures, and we inherited from them this travel bug. I pointed to Ryszard that they were not exactly tourists and their knowledge of other cultures was kind of skewed and one-dimensional, but it did not matter. They travelled, while the rest of our village stayed in their place. On top of that we both emigrated to the West, Ryszard to Canada, me to the UK, although I still lived abroad, while he returned to our village ten years previously, after approximately twenty years spent in Toronto, following the collapse of his marriage and loss of his job. This was, however, something he did not like to ponder. As Andrew noticed, it is easier to hunt for negativity than to mine it: to see flaws in others than in one's own character. All these commonalities were for Ryszard a reason that we should travel together, throwing all the negativity which lent itself to our gaze into one pot, to be spiced and heated, like a witch's cauldron.

When I told him that I'm not like him - I didn't need to prop myself up with other people's misfortune, he looked at me ironically, as if he knew that it was bullshit. At best I fooled myself; at worst I tried to fool others and it was always better to live in truth.

And now, the thought that Ryszard distanced himself from our family, instead of liberating me, made me sad and worried. It felt like his grotesque pursuit of negativity sheltered me from noticing the real negativity, in the world and myself.

Andrew must had read my mind, as he said, 'Ryszard is a creep, but he is our creep. Let's go to him.'

So we took a bottle of wine, pieces of cakes and one Christmas wafer, and cycled to his house. Ryszard was so surprised to see us, and admitted that he had no food for Christmas except for bread, cheese and garlic, which he ate every day. The only Christmas luxury he afforded himself was a lemon, as he liked tea with lemon. He made himself tea with lemon and ate three pieces of cake, while we talked about the weather. He did not bother to share the Christmas wafer with us; he was beyond such nonsense.

We excused ourselves quickly, to return home for Christmas Eve supper.

'What an easy way to score brownie points,' Andrew said when we left.

But it wasn't as easy as we thought. When we returned home, my mother greeted us with reproaches that we left her without telling her where we'd go. And when we confessed that we left to visit Ryszard, she got even angrier, saying that Ryszard offended her deeply when he visited last time. She was so furious that she spent the rest of the evening listing our deficiencies. When she finished, Andrew said:

'You know, granny, who you are?'

'Who?', she asked.

'A Hunter of Negativity. Just like Ryszard.'

PART 2: TOURISTS

Homo Sacer and Her Lover

When Sarah woke up, Thomas was already making coffee and smoking a cigarette. He couldn't live without fags. He seemed to be anxious to even go to sleep, because this would deprive him of his favourite object of consumption, and he smoked straight after they had sex, like a character in films about prostitutes and their clients. But Sarah did not mind it, even liked it, because cigarettes suited him and after sex she wanted to be left alone. Thomas also liked to eat, and his eyes were always on the best risotto or cherry pie in the city. In the past one would call such a man a bon vivant, but these days this term had an archaic inflection, so in her diary she named him 'Agent Cooper'. Despite not paying much attention to his health, in his late forties he still looked good. Probably he even looked better in his forties than in his twenties. For her he looked best when he was naked. Most men look ridiculous without their clothes and they try to hide their shrinking muscles, dicks and balls or try to puff them up by this or that means. Instead, he simply liked to spread himself on the bed, as if unaware of the space he occupied or offered his body as a vessel into which she could escape into a different reality.

This was their sixth meeting in fifteen months and, as before, they met in his apartment in Lindau on Bodensee. He had another apartment in Geneva and a house somewhere in Austria, everywhere with a view of a lake. But he claimed that he was not particularly fond of lakes; it was by accident that he ended up in their proximity. He spent most of his life in Geneva because it was where his children lived and he kept this apartment on Bodensee because he once shared it with his business partner and still liked working there. The house in Austria he inherited from his parents. Lakes were part of his life, but he preferred the sea, because he was into windsurfing and diving. She also used to prefer seas over lakes; the waves crushing on the beach were for her the most beautiful image as they were so dramatic – like Madame Bovary committing her suicide again and again. But these days she did not like drama. Lakes, being quieter, suited her state of mind better. Especially Bodensee; it made her think of an enlarged artery, which is on the verge of breaking, but holds on because it learnt to live in tune with its blood.

They met for the first time in a Budapest hotel, seemingly good, but large and anonymous, where the majority of customers were single people on business trips. The last but one morning before their departure there was a long queue to the breakfast tables and the waiter asked if people wouldn't mind sharing, to speed up the service. They did not mind and so ended up sitting opposite each other and started to talk. He asked if she wanted him to bring her something from the buffet table, which by this point looked like a fortress under siege. Ten minutes later she learnt that he came to Budapest to work on re-designing some buildings in the centre of the city. He specialised in improving what was built badly and travelled all over the world to re-design university campuses, government buildings, even churches. The matter of fact way he explained his work made her think that he was very good at it. She also noticed that his English was faultless; it was only when he pronounced German names one could guess that he came from a German-speaking country.

'Architecture – the favoured discipline of Adolf Hitler,' – she remarked. 'And the only art which neatly connects the past with the future.'

'I'm not exactly Albert Speer,' he replied. 'To start off with, I'm Austrian, not German and my main aim is to salvage as much as possible from the past. I do not like starting from scratch. I do not even know how to do it. I will never bomb the whole city to build a better one in its place. And what do you do for a living?' he asked her.

'I'm an academic. I'm trying to find out how knowledge affects people's moral choices. One might call me a philosopher if not for the fact that what I do is based on empirical research: mostly interviews.'

'Whom do you interview?'

'Mainly people who had to make difficult choices: Holocaust survivors, prisoners, refugees, people who volunteer to endure medical experiments.'

'And what have you discovered?'

'That ignorance is bliss,' she laughed. This was a lie, but it suited her to say it.

'So I should not ask you any more questions?'

'Not today,' she replied.

But he asked her if she was free that day. She was; it was her only free day in Budapest after several days of work. He cancelled his meeting and they went sightseeing, with him as her guide. He knew the city only vaguely, but knew enough about architecture to draw her attention to things, which she would otherwise have ignored. He explained why this bridge was built this way and why this building looked different from another building. He could talk about something specific in neither a superficial nor nerdy way. This was a skill she never mastered herself, therefore never became a public intellectual, despite being highly respected by her peers. Her new acquaintance also knew where to stop off for a coffee, before her feet started to hurt. And from there they returned to the hotel to have sex, as time was in short supply.

He noticed that her room was very messy as for the small number of things she had with her. Her two dresses lay on the bed, rather than hung in the wardrobe, and her remaining two pairs of shoes were distributed evenly between different corners of the room. Several books were lying on the floor, and in one of them her passport served as a book mark. It also looked as if she had some allergy to rubbish bins as orange peel lay near the bed, while an empty bottle stood on the windowsill. She did not apologise for the mess and he found this chaos comforting, as if proof that she would let him go when he wanted to leave. And so it was – they made love and he left for a cigarette. When he returned, she was fast asleep, with her face buried in a pillow. Although Thomas normally respected people's privacy, he took her passport from the book and opened it to check the date of her birth. He was surprised that she was two years older than him, as she looked quite young, but then realised that these days if people look their true age, they must be either sick or poor. Anyway, he was not bothered about his lovers' age. He wondered if he should stay with her till the next morning or go to his room, given that the job was done and his plane was leaving early. He left, packed his things, smoked another cigarette, but then returned to her bed. She clung to his back, sleeping like a child, while he could not fall asleep again, thinking about the cancelled meeting and the calls he needed to make. But mostly he was thinking about the skill with which Sarah handled their bodies; in this she reminded him of his first lover, a Dutch woman almost twenty years older than him, who lived in Vienna at the time. He knew almost nothing about her and she didn't ask him any questions, because this was a condition of what she described as 'zipless fuck'. To fuck zipless, people should not know each other, because knowledge spoils the pleasure. Sarah was also an expert in 'zipless fuck'; no doubt in part thanks to being British. She had to be a posthumous child of the sixties. Austrian and Swiss women could not fuck zipless; for them sex was always a matter of power; they always 'gave' when they took off their clothes, so men were always indebted to them, always in the wrong. (All his wives were Austrian or Swiss).

'Will we meet again?' he asked Sarah in the morning.

'Maybe,' she replied.

'Then let's meet,' he said.

For the meetings she was flexible. She could spend with him a week or so every two or three months, telling at home and at work that she was going on a research trip. She always brought with her a small suitcase with the basics: two sets of clothes suitable to the season, which she never bothered hanging up, two or three books, a small computer, a paper notebook and a small cosmetics bag. What she took, she brought back home. Each of her visits was meant to be a distinct unit. She did not want to leave any traces behind and neither make plans further than the next trip.

During their week together he tried not to work and have his phone switched off, although she did not mind if he worked, met people or took calls. She herself always did some work, making notes on the margins of her books or tapping at the computer. But still it felt like they had plenty of time, maybe because she did not like to do much. Walking to the lake or the city to buy some food, or to a café for a cake was enough for her. She did not like restaurants as sitting at a table tired her and waiting for meals got on her nerves. As he was happy to cook, she let him do it and never interfered. She'd tried communal cooking in the past, but it had never worked for her. At supper he would tell her his life story in small, shapely instalments and so she learnt that he was three times married and divorced. Not that he was the marrying type; a wedding was for him not so much a proof of commitment, as a way of putting order into the pool of his girlfriends and rewarding those who were so kind as to bring his children into the world – even if he did not ask them for such a lavish gift. He was almost proud of his numerous marriages and affairs, but not because they testified to his popularity among women, but because he believed they taught him how to love. 'Love is like architecture,' he said, 'one can excel in it only after a long period of apprenticeship,' and he felt like he was finally ready for his Eiffel Tower.

Sarah was laughing, as his idea of love was completely different from hers – his was based on addition; hers was based on subtraction. For her every episode of love meant that her capacity for love got smaller and now there was almost nothing left. This shrinking was reflected in her sleeping habits – after each new romantic disappointment she moved closer to the edge of the bed and curled up like a foetus. Sarah's husband used to it and actually got annoyed when she tried to move closer to the centre of their bed or when her leg or arm got on his way, but Thomas always moved her close to himself and strengthen her limbs. He did it in such a way that she didn't notice it.

Once she told him about this concept of 'homo sacer': somebody who has only his physical life, *zoe*, rather than *bio*, which was a higher form of existence. She wanted to say that when love was concerned, she became homo sacer – there was no life of a higher order left in her. Because of that in her late forties she enjoyed sex like never before. But she didn't tell him that, as Thomas wouldn't agree. He had his own theory about her, which he presented once or twice when they laid naked. He touched her breast and said: 'there is a wound there – we need to heal it,' before kissing her or putting his head there. There was no wound, only a scar, but there was no point to explain it to him – they were meeting to enjoy themselves, not to make each other miserable by relieving some bad memories.

After supper they would listen to music he chose. Sarah was no longer aware what was fashionable, and didn't even know what genre she liked. In her city there was no longer any shop left selling CDs, while YouTube or Spotify were for her like a maze which was impossible to master. When pressed to choose, she suggested 'something on the pop side, but minimalistic, like minimalist techno'. Not that it was her favourite style, but she was afraid of content. Songs about love embarrassed and moved her in equal measure and she didn't want anybody to see it.

He played for her his favourite tracks arranged in personal playlists, as if to convey a certain concept, like a colour, direction or shape. His apartment was full of books about music, and these were not banal biographies of rock stars, but manuals on producing music, and some on Stockhausen and composers she knew nothing about. He said Stockhausen influenced his ideas about architecture and urban design. It also turned out he had a short career as a DJ and one could hazard a guess that if he hadn't become such a good architect, he would have been a professional musician. He belonged to that type of people who have 'natural' talents, although in reality this is to do with having significant capital at the start. Such people, she learnt from her research, had the greatest chance to survive in a concentration camp or after a plane crash.

It was less than two weeks before Christmas and there was a Christmas tree in Thomas's apartment. Maybe because of this time of the year, the routine of their meetings was disturbed. One day Thomas said that the next time Sarah should come to Geneva and meet his children. The next day he said that he would like her to accompany him to his trip to Delhi – he got a large project there and would stay there for two months. He didn't go as far as asking her to leave her husband, but he mentioned that there were advantages in exclusivity and commitment and that there is a good sex beyond 'zipless fuck' and they have passed this stage anyway. When their last night came he did not rush to the kitchen for his fag, but took her in his arms and whispered:

'I feel so good with you. I do not want you to go. I want you to stay with me forever.'

'I feel good too,' she replied, 'but now let me sleep.'

In the morning when she packed her things to go to the airport, as usual she made sure that she did not leave even a toothbrush and discreetly left under the Christmas tree the bracelet encrusted with diamonds he gave her the previous day. She did not want him to have extra regrets and she was not into diamonds anyway.

What Is Love

Twenty years ago they were madly in love. She loved him so much that she left her long-term boyfriend for him and moved to a different city, to live with him. Now there was nothing left from this love, which made her wonder how it happened. As she was an academic, she decided to investigate it as if it was a research problem, the way she was filling grant applications. One had to answer questions 'what?', 'how?' and 'why?' The first task was to provide a definition of love.

She came to the conclusion that for her love happened when one did something for another person not because they would pay her back, but because she wanted the best for them. She did not even mind if in the process she hurt herself. This is how their love began. She sacrificed a lot for him, but she didn't care, it even gave her pleasure. She was sure that he would sacrifice as much for her if a sacrifice was needed. There were other aspects of love, such as physical attraction, shared interests and mutual admiration. At the beginning they ticked all these boxes. For example, there was so much more to their lovemaking than sex and even simple physical contact, like touching each other's hand, made her shiver with excitement and tenderness.

And then he started to lose interest in what supposedly was of interest to both of them. He would stop in the middle of a film they were watching saying it was boring or that he was tired and she had to finish it by herself or, more often, switch it off. They ceased visiting art galleries in a nearby town, as he admitted he was no longer into art. He confessed that the music she played on her computer was not to his taste and he got into the habit of putting on headphones to listen to his favourite radio station. This also gave him an excuse to ignore what she was saying by preventing her saying it in the first place, as there is no point talking to a person with their headphones on. The next step for him was to ignore her even when he had no headphones, even when she was asking him a question. Usually after asking twice, she stopped, thinking that these questions weren't really important or she could find answers by different means. Sometimes, however, she challenged him, asking him why he was ignoring her. His answer was that he did not hear her or even that she did not ask him any questions – she only thought she did it. As usually there were no witnesses, she had no way to prove she was right. And so there was less and less to talk about and every utterance started to sound like an intrusion. Their conversations became very factual: when? what? why? They even took pride in the economy of their exchanges and the respect granted to the partner's privacy. The downside was that they lost touch with each other's lives and most of their knowledge about each other came from conversations with a third person, when they had guests or were paying somebody a visit. In this way she found out that the team he was leading at work was reduced from over thirty people to seven and he learnt that she became a head of an institute. However, as the gap in their knowledge about each other was growing it became difficult to have visitors as they easily noticed that there was something wrong with them. Their social lives became separate and rather limited. After work he would occasionally go to a pub with the people from his work and once a year visited friends who lived in a different part of the country. She socialised mostly during her business trips and through the internet. In her e-mails she focused on children rather than her husband, which was only natural. Her friends and relatives with children did the same.

Limited communication was coupled with limited interaction. He wouldn't do anything for her unless he absolutely had to. When she asked him to pick her up from the airport when she was returning from one of her journeys, he pointed to the availability of taxis. Around the same time she discovered that she got on his nerves. He a problem with tolerating her habits, like her getting colds. Indeed, she often got colds and was coughing in bed for days, even weeks at a time. He told her that he could not sleep with her coughing so loudly, so she moved to their spare room for the duration of her illnesses. He also disapproved of them sleeping under a warm quilt in winter, finding it suffocating. He was himself the type who in winter clears the snow wearing only a T-Shirt and shorts. For some years she tried to survive under a thin quilt, but it resulted in her suffering from colds practically all the way from October till March and so one year she moved to the spare room for the whole winter. He took it as a sign of both her lack of discipline and her sexual frigidity. By this time every sentence he directed to her was filled with exasperation, as if he wanted to tell her: 'Cannot you see how much it costs me to put up with you?' Indeed, he did not even need to talk. It was enough for him to sigh. When he returned home from work, he immediately started to take a deep breath and release the air so loudly that she could hear his sigh upstairs. The trail of his sighs was a trail of her misdemeanours. It usually started in the kitchen, where the cooker was always dirty from some overboiled food (she cooked everything on the highest temperature) and finished in the spare room, where he discovered the most offending items, such as a large pile of women's magazines and a small pile of painkillers, not mentioning the thick quilt on a permanently unmade bed. He did not know that she was also using anti-depressants, but these she never showed to him – they were hidden in the depth of her handbag. She knew that it was best to keep this trail of disgrace intact, because this provided him with a certain routine at home, which gave him a sense of security. By contrast, he got frustrated when his trail was broken, for example when he found their kitchen spotless or instead of the women's magazines there was Joyce's 'Ulysses' on her bedside table. On such occasions he was marching through the house like a hungry lion in his cage, angry that his piece of meat was not provided.

A moment came when there seemed no point to pretend that the old love was still there, only clouded or polluted. It was annihilated, full stop. He did not love her anymore and she reciprocated with unloving him. She decided that there were two ways to solve their predicament. One was to leave him. This would mean accepting that her heart was broken but avoiding it being broken every day, 24/7. The second solution was to put up with it. She chose the second option. Why? Partly because the death of their love was not spectacular, but gradual, like a prolonged illness, to which one has time to get used. She also convinced herself that love was a luxury; other things were more important, like paying off the mortgage and ensuring that their children lived with both parents, at least till they were ready to fly the nest. After all, if love was a basic human right, Amnesty International would devote part of its magazine to the plight of the unloved. Instead, it only published stories of imprisonment and torture. Slow unlove was even avoided in women's magazines, which preferred to publish stories of love or love properly finished by extramarital affairs, divorces and moving on (to a new love).

However, living with unlove day after day was not straight-forward. She had to build for herself a place in which she could find solace. It was a virtual place, and like a spare room she made it into her own room, it was an eclectic and seemingly disorganised place, filled with fragments: images, memories, words. Kitsch ruled there, not because she was particularly keen of kitsch, far from that, but because it was a perfect ignition, allowing her to move swiftly to some deeper (un)reality, where no images, memories or words were needed, one was floating in the immaterial ocean of peace, which was as close to happiness, as she could get in her circumstances. Such a role fulfilled old disco songs, especially Haddaway's 'What Is Love'. When she arrived at work, cold and miserable not only from her daily injection of unlove, but also the dark winter and long commute, she sat at her desk, closed her eyes and allowed the energetic music play in her head and soon she found herself in her shapeless nirvana, where she was not even a full person, but a bundle of pleasant sensations. However, it was not easy to hold a grip on the real world, while dwelling in a dreamworld because the real, being so cold and unjust, kept pushing her away. She felt most lonely among her children, because in front of them she had to pretend that she and their dad were happy together and there were days when even Haddaway could not guide her to happiness. During such days she cried and prayed that her suffering would soon be over, brought on by terminal cancer or a car accident. Unfortunately, her numerous pains and colds did not translate into any more substantial illnesses and she was a very careful driver.

Throughout most of the years of their unlove she believed it was possible for them to make the return journey; regain the old love bit by bit or at least salvage something from what they had at the beginning. The truth was that they tried several times, usually on her initiative. On such occasions, she made certain rules for them, which they both were meant to obey, like focusing on the little which they still had in common and simultaneously looking for something which might be added to this short list of shared properties. He promised to stop wearing headphones at home and answer all her questions. She agreed to wear warm pyjamas in winter, so there was no need for them to use a thick quilt, and promised to cook soup on a lower temperature as soon as it started simmering. They made plans to see exhibitions and go to concerts. But their attempts did not work. Old habits kicked in. He discovered that he had an important document to prepare over the weekend, which left no time for visiting a gallery. Plus the old exasperation resurfaced in his voice the day after they promised each other patience and respect.

The last time they tried to recapture the missing love was after she had an affair. She did not plan to have any lovers as she believed that only monogamy was compatible with love as she understood it. But life took her by surprise; she met her lover in a hotel, on one of her business trips and he proved irresistible. They went to bed the same day and after that she started to visit him every six weeks or so in his summer house on Bodensee. Although he came from a country not particularly known for advancing the feminist cause, he seemed to have a natural affinity for women. He liked doing things for her, like cooking, making coffee and finding music she might enjoy. He liked the way she talked, maybe on account of her foreign accent. She liked his perfect body when in the morning he was sat on chair naked, except for his boxer shorts and Swiss watch. She was thinking that in her country men of this kind did not exist or maybe they all emigrated to Hollywood. But most of all she liked the fact that he seemed to like the way she was. She expected it would not last, but for time being, being with her lover was even better than dwelling in her dreamworld. And then he told her that he wanted them to be properly together, day after day, so she split with him as she knew what would be the most likely outcome, if she agreed to his proposal. Although she was convinced that she made the right decision, her heart was bleeding. She was crying more than before and had to go to the doctor to get stronger anti-depressants.

She did not tell her husband about her affair, not so much because she wanted to hide this fact from him, but because by this point they stopped discussing any intimacies. But he must have felt that she found a way out of her predicament, as he suddenly changed his tack. He stopped sighing and proposed that in spring they go on a holiday together, without the children. Besides, by this point there were no children to go with them, as their youngest had moved out of the house several months earlier.

They went to a resort, of the sort with a blue sky, sandy beach and free drinks. The following day after their arrival he proposed that they go for a walk in the sunset and took her hand. It was a shock for her, as by this point she'd forgotten his touch and it triggered the memory of the walks with her lover. She could not stand it and gently pulled her hand out of his grip and put it in the pocket of her shorts. After that there was no more evening walks. But apart from this episode, it was a good holiday, largely on the account of the drinks and the sea. She never swam so much since her teenage years. Every day she swam further and further, leaving him on the beach, looking after their possessions and then she took over, freeing him to swim too. The last day before their return, she was sad at the thought of returning home and after lunch, unusually for her, she drank three alcoholic cocktails. Then she went for her usual swim. After some time she noticed that she lost some of her strength and the shore was far away and it would require an extra effort to make it to the beach. Normally there were some boats to patrol the coast, but on this occasion she could not see them. She changed her position, moving onto her back, but the result was that she lost a sense of direction and swam away from the shore. She changed again, but in the process drank some salty water as quite a big wave came at her. It made her very weak and she realised that she would drown. And then she noticed that somebody was swimming towards her. Was it him? To find out, she called his name.

A Good Holiday

Barbara had to save money all year round so her son could have a good holiday. This meant going with him for two weeks somewhere abroad and sending him to a school camp abroad for another two weeks. The rest of the summer vacation Adam spent on short trips in Poland with Barbara or his grandmother. This year, however, Barbara waited too long for a good deal to Spain or Croatia and, in the end, there were no good deals, even for Bulgaria, so she decided to take Adam to Sopot at the Baltic Coast, where they were before, but only on a short excursion.

They arrived in Sopot with no problems, but Adam wasn't happy about their hotel room, which was small and didn't have a sea view, but overlooked the bins at the back of the hotel, A much greater disappointment, however, came the next morning, when they went to the beach, only to discover that swimming was forbidden due to the high level of algae. They went to the lifeguards to find out when the sea would be open again for swimming, and learnt that for this to happen, the temperature would have to go down at least five degrees and there would have to be strong wind to wash away the algae. This, most likely, wouldn't happen in the next four to five days. The information gleaned from the internet was even more pessimistic. The beach hygiene inspector, interviewed for the local newspaper, predicted that the Gdansk Bay wouldn't be swimmable this summer at all. This was, inevitably, used as a reason to demand more resources from the central government to clean up the beach.

'What's the point of going to the seaside, if you can't swim?' asked Adam rhetorically.

'Yes, what's the point,' agreed Barbara.

She went to the hotel reception to enquire about the nearest place open to swimmers.

'Władysławowo' said the receptionist.

'How far is Władysławowo?' asked Barbara.

'Two and a half hours by train, if you are lucky,' he replied with the aura of an Yorkshireman from the famous Monty Python sketch. 'It would probably be faster to fly to Riga, where there's no algae, as far as I am aware, if you want to swim the Baltic sea.'

'So what you suggest we do?' asked Barbara.

'There is plenty to do in Sopot: several nightclubs, the summer market, poetry and jazz festivals. A small beer festival will open in Gdynia next week.'

There was no point in saying that all these attractions would not appeal to her twelve-year old son, so she thanked the receptionist, returned to their room and said to Adam: 'Let's go to Władysławowo. This is the nearest place where we can swim in the sea.'

'Okay', said Adam.

They packed quickly and took a taxi to the station in order not to miss the train which was leaving in less than half an hour.

The train was old-fashioned and very slow, stopping at every village they were passing, which made Adam grumble.

'It will be nighttime by the time we arrive in Władysławowo. When we are going to swim?' he asked accusingly.

'I'm trying my best,' said Barbara. 'Try to read. Your Polish teacher complains that you are not reading anything. Now you have an opportunity to prove her wrong.'

'The books you buy me are boring,' Adam said.

'So buy those which you like,' replied Barbara. 'If you want, tomorrow we can go to Gdansk and do a tour of the bookshops. Apparently, Gdansk is great for second-hand bookshops.'

Barbara couldn't focus on her book either and the train was getting on her nerves too. She couldn't believe that trains could be so slow in the twenty-first century.

But eventually they arrived. The town turned out to be quite large and it took them fifteen minutes or so to get to the beach. The beach was very long, very wide and packed with people. Most of them surrounded themselves with folded screens. This must have been a particularly Polish custom, as Barbara never saw them in other countries. Some people joined two or three screens, grabbing for themselves a large piece of the beach. Others sat in enormous wicker chairs. These contraptions left little space for new arrivals and obscured the view.

Adam looked at his mother with his eyes wide open and mouth compressed. Barbara knew what it meant – he wasn't happy with the place, but he wasn't going to complain.

After walking for a couple of minutes they found a place next to a water sports rental. It was a bright yellow shack, which could be seen from far away.

'In case you get lost or whatever, remember that we are here, near this yellow shack,' she said to Adam.

They put their towels down next to a nice looking and screen-free family with two kids, who promised to look after their stuff, when they went swimming. Barbara took out from her bag a sandwich with cheese, made at breakfast and asked

Adam if he wanted to eat it, but he looked at it with scorn. He didn't like home-prepared food and, especially, he didn't like to carry it and others to see that they are the sort of people who make their own sandwiches. .

Then they went to swim, as it was already well after 3 o'clock. The water was cooler than on the Costa Del Sol, where they were the previous year, but this was to be expected from the Baltic Sea. The advantage was that nobody was whistling at them when they were swimming. They were both good swimmers so they liked to swim further, leaving the crowd of waders behind. On the way back, Adam stayed in shallow water for a long time, with his head in the water and legs doing scissors in the air. He started doing it when he was four or five years old and it became his holiday signature.

Eventually there was time to go out and find something to eat. Barbara led them through the tight forest of beach chairs and screens and when she reached their towels, she noticed that Adam wasn't following her. How could it be? She quickly retrieved her steps, returning to the place where they left the water. Some kids playing with inflatables that she noticed before were still there. She asked them if they'd seen Adam and one had, but he hadn't paid attention to where he went. She walked up and down the beach, looking at boys in red swimming trunks and there was one some distance away, but it wasn't Adam. He must have returned to their place. But he wasn't there either.

'What shall I do?' asked Barbara the family which was looking after their belongings.

'Go to the lifeguard,' said the father. 'He has binoculars and would see any child swimming on his own.'

Barbara put her dress on quickly and ran to the lifeguard's 'nest' which was pretty far away. But there was no lifeguard there; his working hours were 8 a.m. to 4.p.m. and it was already after 4.

'My son is lost. What should I do?' asked Barbara, partly to herself, partly to the people who were standing nearby.

'Go to the police', one man said.

'Where is the police station?' asked Barbara.

'It must be somewhere in the centre,' he said, looking at his Google Maps. 'Here,' he said, showing her.

Barbara returned to her towels, took her bag and ran. The family asked her for her phone number, so they could phone her in case Adam returned.

It took Barbara some time to explain at the station what had happened, but once the information was taken down, the police acted swiftly. They mobilised all forces available in the twenty-kilometres radius. Suddenly there were plenty of men in uniforms on the beach and police cars were passing in all directions.

'If we don't find him in the next hour or so, we will use a helicopter,' said the officer in charge.

Fifteen minutes had passed and Adam was found. He was sitting in a café at the other side of the beach, drinking orange juice and waiting to be found.

'How have you ended up here?' asked Barbara. 'Why didn't you follow me when we were returning to our spot on the beach?'

'I followed you, but you were walking so fast that I wasn't able to keep up and when I shouted to you to slow down, you ignored me,' said Adam. 'So I returned to the sea and walked on the shore till the end of the beach, thinking that you would find me on one end of the beach or the other.'

'But this was the wrong end of the beach,' said Barbara,

'I know that now,' said Adam.

'I told you to look for a yellow shack in case you get lost.'

'I don't remember you saying it,' said Adam.

There was no point to continue this discussion, especially as the police officer asked them to go to the station as he needed to write a report. Barbara noticed that the guy was good-looking or rather it occurred to her that she would notice it, if not for the fact that such an observation was completely irrelevant.

At the station he turned to Adam and said: 'Can you go to the other room, please, with this lady. I need to talk to your mum on my own.'

When Adam left, the policeman said: 'It is great news that your son was found. Now, however, we need to follow due procedures. According to the law, you committed an act of a serious neglect of a child.'

'I haven't neglected him, he got lost,' protested Barbara.

'This is how you see it and how you can present the matter in the court.'

'What will happen to me?' she asked.

'In the best case you get a social worker overseeing the child's situation at home for some time, to make sure nothing like that happens again. In the worst case, you lose, hopefully temporarily, your parental rights. And you will have to cover the costs of using the resources of the police, which amounted to eight police cars and thirty people.'

'So, if there was a helicopter, I will have to pay for a helicopter?' asked Barbara with a hint of sarcasm.

'I'm afraid so,' said the officer.

'I thought the police is there to help citizens, not to extract money from them. Pity you didn't tell me all these things in advance so maybe I would look for my son by myself. Would be cheaper,' she continued, suppressing tears.

'Perhaps. But what would happen if you didn't find him till the evening or till tomorrow?' he asked. And added after a while: 'We will also need to inform Adam's father. Can you provide me with his name, address and telephone number?'

'Adam has no father. I'm raising him on my own.'

For some reason, by this point the tears started to fall down her cheeks. This made Barbara angry, as it looked as if she was sorry about being a single mother.

The policeman looked at her for a while, and then at his computer, where he was checking something for couple of minutes. Barbara thought that he would say something to add to her humiliation, but instead he got up, put his hand on her shoulder and said: 'Okay. I get it. You think life is unfair and all men are bastards. You are right, but sometimes there are exceptions to the rule. You can leave now and there will be no charges. And you are lucky that we didn't call a helicopter because its costs would be more difficult to erase.'

Then they went to the room, where Adam was sitting with a policewoman watching something on YouTube. He turned to her: 'The case is closed. Adam, you can leave now with your mum. Next time when you go on the beach bring a skipping rope and when you go somewhere, keep one end and give the other to your mum.'

'Thank you,' said Barbara, holding Adam's hand.

When they left the police station, Barbara realised that she had cramps in her stomach. If she was so hungry, how hungry Adam must had been? But it was difficult to find a restaurant which would suit them. Eventually they settled for a huge, barn-like place with open gates and large wooden benches. It was darkish, played loud music and had the anonymity of a motel, which suited them, as they didn't want anybody to pay attention to them.

Adam ordered a large pizza and Coca Cola and Barbara got herself a roll with some salads and a small beer. Despite the hunger, she couldn't eat much, but the beer made her feel better or at least woke her up from the shock in which she'd been since Adam's vanishing. She started to notice people around her. There were many families with children, some bikers in leather jackets and ridiculous hairstyles and teenage girls playing on their mobile phones. Most of them were eating pizzas, leaving the crusty bits on their plates. This was also the way Adam was eating his pizza. Barbara couldn't understand such wastefulness. She put her roll in a plastic bag and slipped it into her handbag and ate the remnants off Adam's plate.

'As your grandma said, capitalism corrupted Poles. Before the war they would collect every crumb of bread from the floor, and kissed it before eating it,' she said.

'How granny could know how people ate their pizza before the war if she was born after the war?'

'Maybe she read it in the books. The point is that people should eat everything what they order,' said Barbara. 'Otherwise food is wasted, animals are killed and tropical forests are cut down in vein.'

'Just because of some pizza crust being uneaten?' asked Adam.

'That's right. Precisely.'

There was no more food to be eaten and it was time to catch the last train to Sopot. At the station it turned out that the train was a bit delayed, so Barbara agreed to go to a kiosk nearby selling waffles with different toppings and she bought Adam a waffle with whipped cream and strawberry jam. She asked him to carry it properly so he wouldn't make a mess of it. But when they were taking their seats on the train Adam lost control of the waffle. It made a pirouette in the air and pieces of it landed on Adam's clothes, Barbara's, a woman sitting next to Adam, the chairs and the floor. It seemed like everything around them was covered in red and white grease, like in a Laurel and Hardy film or some other slapstick comedy. Barbara, however, wasn't in a mood for laughing. She abruptly took the remnants of the waffle from his hand, threw it into a bin and started to shout:

'Why did you ask me to buy you a waffle if you don't know how to eat it? Why couldn't you keep the waffle firmly in your hand as I told you? Why do you always ignore what I tell you?'

She was hitting a small folded table located between them with her fist, which made Adam jump in his seat. She knew they looked ridiculous, like an exotic band trying to produce rhythm, using nonstandard instruments, but she couldn't stop, even though Adam was crying and meekly pleading: 'Mum, please, stop, people are looking at us.'

'I don't care about people,' shouted Barbara, hitting the table for the last time as she broke it.

The middle-aged woman who sat next to Adam said to Barbara:

'You shouldn't talk to your son like that. He is only a child.'

An older man, standing next to their seat, joined in the conversation, saying to Barbara: 'You are mentally unstable. People like you shouldn't be allowed to look after children. He would be better off with foster parents or in an orphanage.'

'Yes, yes,' added a small choir of mostly female voices.

But then a man sitting in a parallel row said to Barbara's critics: 'Leave the poor woman in peace. I saw her earlier. Her son got lost on the beach today. There was police looking for him. She had enough stresses for one day.'

'Perhaps the kid didn't get lost, but run away from such a wicked mother,' one woman replied.

Barbara felt too ashamed and humiliated to talk back. Despite the train being overcrowded, they left the carriage and went to the other end of the train, where, after two stops, they found two free seats near the window. It seemed like nobody there knew them, but in order not to be recognised, they spent the rest of the journey looking at the landscape which they were passing, although shortly there was no landscape to look at, only darkness, as if the world wanted them to face each other.

When they arrived in their hotel it was almost midnight, but they couldn't fall sleep. Each was crying in their bed, without uttering a word. Only after an hour or so Adam said: 'Mum, do you love me? Do you regret that I was born?'

It was some time till Barbara replied, as tears and phlegm in her throat suffocated her and made her temporarily mute. Eventually, when she overcame it, she said:

'I love you. I don't regret that you were born. You are everything I have. I just wish you stopped daydreaming and were more present in this world. I could lose you twice today. You could be kidnapped by some pedophile or the police might have recommended that I was not fit to look after you and the social services might have taken you from me. Such things happen. You can read in newspapers about mothers who lose their kids because they were poor or were caught drunk or something.'

'But you are not poor or a drunkard.'

'If I lose my job we become poor. Life is not so easy for me. Maybe it is time you realise it rather than criticising everything I do.'

'I don't criticise everything,'

'Not everything, but a lot.'

'I'm sorry. Can I come to your bed now?'

'Of course you can.'

In the morning Barbara looked at the flights from Gdansk and there was one super-offer to Venice leaving in the afternoon; it was about 200 Euros for both of them return. She booked it immediately, together with a hotel. Then she woke Adam up and said: 'We are going to Italy today. There is plenty of sea there, so if there are algae somewhere or if we don't like one place we can go to another one.'

After a short discussion the hotel manager agreed to refund half of their cost. They packed their luggage and went to the airport. Several hours later they arrived in the hotel with a view of the canal and a row of colourful houses. They left their luggage and went for a walk:

'Mum, this is the most beautiful place I ever saw,' said Adam.

'Yes, I think nothing on Earth is more beautiful than Venice. At least nothing human-made. Strange that centuries have passed since Venice was built, but nothing better was built in the meantime,' she replied.

She thought that she also wouldn't exceed the best moments of her life. Things would only get worse, for humanity and for her. Success would mean avoiding disaster, not reaching some peak. Heaven had a ceiling; hell was bottomless. But she didn't want to talk about it with Adam.

'Let's go for a pizza. There is no better place to have pizza than Italy,' she said instead. 'Tomorrow we will go to a beach where I was on my first trip to Venice fifteen years ago. Maybe we will have a good holiday, after all.'

The Grand Dad

Tuesday

On holidays we try to dine in restaurants serving local people. Not only is the food better and cheaper than in those geared towards tourists, but also once the food is brought, the customers are left to their own devices. There is no pressure to engage in conversation with the waiters, order more food than one is able to eat or drink local alcohol at the end of the meal. Unfortunately, in this small resort on Crete, where we came for Andrew's autumn half-term, there were no restaurants for the locals. All tavernas were located at the sea front, with an eye on the passing holidaymakers, so we chose the first one. Apart from us, there was only a middle-aged couple finishing their meal. They sat at the porch, while we decided to take a table in the higher part, the 'restaurant proper', as it felt too cold and spooky to sit so close to the sea which in the dark looked menacing. However, it turned out to be spooky also in our part, not least because the place was poorly lit, and the two neighbouring tavernas were already closed down for winter.

Only two people were working in the restaurant: the waiter, who introduced himself as Dimitris, and his wife, who was the chef. Although we did not expect to eat much, conscious that these people kept the restaurant open only for us, we ended up ordering a huge quantity of food and staying there almost till midnight. When we were leaving, I heard a weak crying, as of a child, coming from the kitchen, but assumed that it was merely a voice in my head or of some cats passing nearby.

The village was full of stray cats, but we did not have any food for them.. Still, they appreciated our petting, if only as a means to a goal which was not fulfilled. Among them were three, which we subsequently befriended, a tubby one with pupils of different colours, whom I named Bowie, a fluffy ginger one, which was hobbling because of a disfigured front paw, whom I gave a Polish name Kuśtyczka, as it sounded more tender than the English Hobbler and one who was multi-coloured, whom Andrew called Rainbow.

Back in the hotel, we agreed that the food in the restaurant was fresh, inexpensive, and tasted of home cooking. We also liked Dimitris. Although he was excessively friendly, shaking hands of all three of us and presenting himself as an Anglophile, despite not ever having been to England, and later confessing to meeting many nice people from Poland, there was innocence and honesty to his demeanour. His slim face and short body were those of a man affected by heavy work and worry, yet one who did not give into despair, anger or apathy. His sunny personality was reflected in his use of English. For example, the volcano on the island opposite Crete was in his idiom 'lively' rather than 'active'. He also knew a lot of awe-inspiring adjectives, such as 'stupendous', 'splendid', 'marvellous', 'stunning', 'fabulous' and 'grand' and often used several in the same sentence for a stronger effect. Most of them referred to the beauty of Crete, but he was also generous in describing people. In England such a manner of talking annoyed me, but on this occasion it amused me, due to the fact that many things we accept in foreign cultures simply because they are foreign.

Wednesday

Before Michael and Andrew got up in the morning, I went for a stroll. The main road, was quite steep, as the village was surrounded by hills, covered by white and blue hotels and villas, small gardens and olive orchards, and patches of nondescript greenery. The only vegetables I could see were cabbage, onion and dill. I was first surprised that there was so little variety of vegetables, but then realised that this was also true about my home village in Poland. People in such places stopped producing anything, because nothing was profitable any more. These vegetables, plus potatoes and tomatoes, also dominated on the shelves of the three local supermarkets. The furthest of them got the best supplies. I bought there a large bag of dry cat food, tuna-flavoured, with the intent of deepening my bond with Bowie, Kuśtyczka and Rainbow. Near the end of the main road there was a school. There were very few children in classes as most of the benches were empty. This also reminded me of my home village, where children became a rarity. The last building on this road was a small church.

When I returned, Michael tried to make Andrew get up and go for breakfast, despite the fact that I bought some food to eat in the apartment. In the breakfast room, only three tables were taken. Apart from us there was a French family with two children, who stayed in the apartment next to us, and two youngish Finnish women. We learnt that the Finnish women and the French family were leaving before us, making us the last guests in the hotel this season. The breakfast was disappointing, with soggy cornflakes, which made Andrew angry, as few things he disliked more than getting up early for such a trivial reason as a free substandard breakfast. He made a pledge never to eat hotel food again. When we were about to leave, the owner, an energetic woman in her forties, approached us asking if we would not mind if the swimming pool was emptied one day before our departure and Michael agreed on behalf of all of us..

Andrew and Michael were meant to go diving that day, but their trip was cancelled due to wind. Instead, we all went to the beach, but it wasn't a good day for sunbathing either - the sun was hidden behind the clouds and the wind was pushing the clouds in the wrong direction. On top of that, Andrew complained about excessive amount of sand and after swimming he was shivering and wanted to return to the hotel, to get rid of the sand which was hurting him.

Before we left, I took a good look at the people around us. These were families with pre-school children and pensioners, taking advantage of their freedom to holiday on the cheap. But for many it felt like the advantage was not great. Older women lay on deckchairs, covered with bath robes, looking like seals brought to the shore against their will. Older men were sitting reading newspapers, trying not to look bored, although counting the hours until lunch or a coffee break. Only the children and some parents seemed at ease, playing in the sand with buckets and spades. The image was mildly depressing, but mostly banal, and as usual in such a situation I wondered if this banality was the reality or my lazy eye. Would Thomas Mann, whose 'Death in Venice' I carried in my bag, see the sea so sea-like and the children so childlike?

For lunch we went to the same restaurant as the previous evening. On this visit we noticed that the name of the restaurant was 'Cochili' – 'Shells'. This was the least pretentious name of the restaurants we passed; others wooed holidaymakers with names such as 'Acropolis', 'Olympus', 'Socrates', 'Zorba' or 'Greek Paradise'. Shells were also the only ornament in the interior of 'Cochili', which was fine for us, given that it had much natural beauty thanks to its location and an abundance of plants which enveloped its thin, wooden walls and columns.

Dimitris greeted us with the same friendliness as the day before, yet tainted by guilt, as it was clear that he had less time for us, given that five tables were taken, which put him and his wife under a lot of pressure. One table were taken by a German family, who reproached him for not being able to provide them with all dishes which were listed on the menu. Other families were complaining about the stray cats entering the premises, which – according to the mother – was unhygienic and unpleasant for her kids. I was on the verge of telling off the woman, but Andrew stopped me. 'Just choose your food, mum,' he said. Too few staff or too many customers was not the only problem for Dimitris and his wife. Another was locked in a pen in the corner of the main part of the restaurant, near the kitchen. It was a boy about three years old; his presence explained why I was hearing cries the previous night. The boy busied himself with a mobile phone on which he was watching cartoons. Whenever Dimitris walked past the pen, he greeted the boy with his guilty smile. His wife couldn't even do as much as she was locked in the kitchen, juggling the preparation of at least ten different dishes. I thought that the boy was Dimitris' grandson and I pictured a young, irresponsible couple who left their child behind, when going on vacation. Michael, however, thought that he was his father.

Although we weren't the last to arrive for lunch, we were the last to be served. Dimitris apologised but said that he first wanted to get rid of the other customers. He added that this day was an anniversary of Greece's liberation from Germany, but it felt like his country was more in bondage to Germans than ever. At least he managed to put a Greek flag on the table of these pesky Germans. I was not sure if they noticed and even if so, whether they got the symbolism of his act. It was only when all guests except us had left that the couple took the boy out of his pen and started to take care of him, giving him food and talking to him. One could then see how affectionate they were and how intelligent was the boy. He was even slightly bilingual, greeting us in English and being able to name a couple of things in this language. Eventually Dimitris took him to our table and lifted him up, saying 'Nikolaus, my son,' as if wanting to quash any doubts we might have had about his virility or age.

We took a stroll after lunch and noticed that the front of one of the closed restaurants was taken by a family of cats: two adults and five kittens. Andrew was convinced that it was a mother and father and their kids, even though I never saw a cat's family in which a father was present. However, the adults seemed to have different characters and roles within the family. The white fluffy female was patient and easy going, allowing the little ones to suckle her as she was standing with her paws rested on the metal gate, looking at the sea melancholically, as if pondering on her lot. The other one, black, short-haired and muscular, was swift and nervous, constantly circling the kittens, as if making sure that they avoided any mischief, and punished them when they misbehaved. Andrew was not too impressed by his behaviour, but he said: 'At least he is around.'

Thursday

We left in the morning for Heraklion. It was meant to be a beautiful city with impressive Venetian buildings dominating the port, but its beauty was overshadowed by a large bus station nearby. I don't like such stations, as they tend to be full of drafts; information there is difficult to obtain, staff is unfriendly and it is easy to get one's legs bruised by somebody's bulky bag. A large bus station in the centre of the town also typically means that there are no trains in such a place, rendering it claustrophobic.

Michael insisted we start by visiting the main historical museum, as he always did, when we went abroad, even though neither Andrew nor myself liked museums. For Andrew, they were like obstacle courses, with no extra points for running fast and a visit to the toiletbeing the only reward for completing them. For me, they were glorified junk shops, in which even the greatest objects of art looked abandoned. But Michael liked them; for him they were a tool to learn about history and a way to imagine a better present. This museum, covering over five thousand years of the island's history, felt even more like a junk-shop than what we usually saw, with half of the exhibits looking like poor copies of the souvenirs displayed on the stalls we passed on the way to it.

Afterwards we had lunch in what looked like a trendy part of the city. Sitting at a table outside we observed people passing by and noticed that all young Greeks wore beards. These were not beards growing in place of balding heads, which were so common among northern men, but in excess of hairy scalps. All men were slim and had very good postures, as if their heads tried to reach Mount Olympus. Andrew noticed that some of these men looked like images of Greek philosophers in his philosophy textbook. Those with shorter beards, longer noses and greatest sex-appeal he labelled Aristotles; the stouter and less attractive Socrateses.

'Everything changes, but people stay the same,'said Michael, commenting on our little game.

Andrew smiled, with a whiff of derision, which appeared frequently when he was listening to his father peddling banalities.

'Those left behind stay the same, those who move on, change,' he said. 'At least these Greeks here do not mind being left behind.'

Our waiter also had a beard, as well as his two friends who smoked and ate with him. The food tasted good, but was less distinct, with pieces of courgettes and aubergines all having the same shape and size, unlike in 'Cochili', where they were slightly misshaped.

From the balcony in our hotel we had a view on a large square, neighbouring a parking lot. It looked like a theatre stage, with cats rehearsing for a play. Although I was tired from the trip to Heraklion, in the evening I went tor a walk to feed them. Bowie, Kuśtyczka and Rainbow were there, and they brought a whole regiment of their friends, including some kittens with huge shiny eyes on triangular faces, which in darkness looked like the faces of alien creatures. By this point I could capture the differences in their character. Bowie, true to his name, was not really interested in food and tried to mesmerise me with his gaze. Kuśtyczka made up for her disability with agility. She was even able to scoop food with her crooked paw. 'Like a Pole, always making up for the historical deficiencies, 'Andrew would say the next day. Rainbow, on the other hand, like an archetypal English person, did not seek any favours and was neither humble not arrogant and his natural neutrality was unique in the crowd of cats trying to transcend the crowd.

There was somebody observing me from a balcony of our hotel - the son of our French neighbours. He came down to help. My French was limited and rusty, but I learnt that his name was Luc, he lived in Normandy and had no pets at home. Despite that, he knew how to handle cats. He did not pick them and was attentive to their needs, trying to shelter Kuśty-czka and make sure that the slower and gentler ones were not outsmarted by the quick and aggressive. By the end of our feeding session, almost half of the bag of cat food wasgone , and Luc became very talkative. We agreed to meet the next eve-ning in the same place. While feeding the cats I was checking whether 'Cochili' had any customers. Three tables were taken, which seemed to be a good number for Dimitris and his wife. Back in the room, I could not help but keep checking from our balcony if the guests had finished, but it was only at one in the morning when I saw the lights in 'Cochili' being switched off and then Dimitris carrying his sleeping son in his arms to the car, with his wife following them with a large cotton bag. They looked like Joseph and Mary, carrying baby Jesus tired, yet defiant.

Friday

Michael and Andrew left the hotel early in the morning to go on a diving expedition, which meant that I had the whole apartment to myself. As soon as they left I turned up the volume of my music, starting with Lesley Gore's 'You Don't Own Me' and 'It's My Party'. But the music ultimately left me sad, so I switched to more neutral electronic stuff, packed my bag with cat food and left. I fed first those congregating near the hotel and then went further, in search of more needy creatures.

As I was passing the sea front, the first holiday martyrs appeared on the beach, the cafés' owners began sweeping sand from their part of the road and a small group of holidaymakers congregated waiting for them to finish their job, chatting and laughing.

Walking up the steep hill was tiring and the road to the furthest supermarket felt twice as long as before. I planned to buy more cat food, but the shop was closed and a notice on the door announced in English that it would reopen next April. The two remaining grocery shops did not have any dry food for cats, only tins, which I did not buy, as insufficiently processed meat made me nauseous. Instead, I stuffed my bag with cheap sausages and cheese. There was not much else to buy in the village. The two clothes shops on the high street were selling only a few beach dresses, discoloured tracksuits and vests embroidered with silver and gold, fashionable twenty years previously. More scattered shops with souvenirs and jewellery advertised themselves as selling hand-made things, but apart from some olive-based soaps and wooden spoons, all of them appeared to be mass-produced in China. On the way back to the hotel I stopped at the place where the cat family lived. Both parents were there and it turned out that both were mothers, as both were being milked by the kittens. However, the one whom we took for the father was clearly doing it reluctantly, as she kept changing her position and trying to get rid of one of the kittens. I was wondering whether to tell Andrew about my discovery, as he could not reconcile himself to the fact that there was so little use for males in the natural world.

I was tempted to go back to bed, but the sun was shining and I knew that if I fell asleep, I would be awake most of the night. I changed into a swimming costume and went to the beach and almost straight to the water. It was pleasant to swim, but I did not go far, turning back some twenty metres before the buoys. I swam fast and nervously, as the fear of drowning overwhelmed and embarrassed me. Ironically, when I reached the shore, an older woman, who was lying on a deckchair next to me, told me that she was impressed by my courage to swim so far. She confessed that she did not properly swim even once in this resort – every day she put her feet into the water, but turned back immediately. Her husband smiled, adding that this was always the case with her – the water had to be 25 C for her to swim. They had to be from the South, I gathered, to have such high expectations. Indeed, they were from Italy. I also assumed that they were pensioners, but it turned out that they were still in more than full-time employment, owning a hotel in a ski resort and making the most of their own out-of-season vacation. Their names were Annabella and Sergio.

Being themselves professionals in the tourism industry, they were very critical about the quality of service in this place. What got particularly on their nerves was that, as opposed to treating the last tourists with extra respect, as they were pro-longing their business, the Greeks regarded them as an obstacle to closing the place down. They had a point – as we were speaking some workers were collecting deckchairs from the beach and packing them up into a van. They left only those which were in use so that when a new person arrived, there were no more deckchairs for them. This was the reason Anna-bella was anxious to leave the beach, as she was in no mood to put her pristine towel straight on the sand. Yet, the couple decided to leave after all, asking me to join them for a coffee. But I stayed to finish my book and to be there for the return of the boat which took Michael and Andrew for their diving trip. It was a unique opportunity for me to play Penelope in the original ambience.

Michael and Andrew arrived safely and keen to tell me about all the things they saw deep in the water, including two octopuses and masses of plastic. But it was not everything. They were diving with another couple, consisting of father and son, who invited all three of us for supper in the neighbouring village, in a restaurant which was apparently the best this side of Heraklion. Being invited was such a rare event that Michael couldn't refuse. It meant that we had to limit ourselves to a lunch in 'Cochili' and not to overeat, as the supper was meant to be rather early. Dimitris was happy to see us, saying that his wife prepared for me something special – a cabbage roll, to make up for the lack of vine rolls, which were still on the menu, but not in the kitchen. Unfortunately, it was filled with meat, as its Polish sister dish, so it was not suitable for me. I was sorry to disappoint him and he had a guilty expression when bringing me the usual grilled vegetables, even though I reassured him that they were delicious. I looked at the pen, where normally Nikolaus sat with his mobile phone, but it was empty. I asked Dimitris where his son was and he replied that his wife's sister was looking after him, as the boy got a bit of temperature. Everything seemed to be as the other day, but it was clear that Dimitris was distracted and his natural friendliness became somewhat robotic. He didn't even protest when we refused the obligatory raki and grapes. I thought it was even a good coincidence that we had supper arranged elsewhere.

In some ways the father and son, with whom we went for supper, were like a mirror reflection of Michael and Andrew. They came here because of the diving facilities and they travelled all over the world testing different waters; the difference was that they gravitated towards Africa and Australia, while

Michael and Andrew favoured the Caribbean and India. The father was a doctor, like Michael and the son was two years younger than Andrew. Both were the only children of their fathers.

The father was a nice and handsome guy with an almost Mediterranean look and a non-German accent, suggesting that he lived abroad. The son, by contrast, fit perfectly the Aryan ideal, having blond hair and pale complexion, most likely inherited from his absent mother. He was a very pretty boy, yet shy and not comfortable to endure a long conversation in English – a language he did not know well, to his father's disappointment. While his beauty rendered him close to Tadzio from Mann's novella, his behaviour was opposite. He was not brought up to be a member of the aristocracy, perfecting the art of being idle and feeling superior over peers, but of the middle class, taught to be active at all cost. He also seemed less capable than Andrew to resist the pressure of doing something. He looked to me like the perfect material to end up a failure. In this company I mattered little, as is usually the case when the only woman among the men is middle-aged. My only role was to step in when the men exhausted the stories about different types of seals, octopuses and coral reefs, encountered during their exotic trips. There were many such trips to share, so I stayed quiet, only correcting small details in Michael's accounts, not to be pedantic, but to show that I listen and paid attention.

The restaurant was called 'Blue Lobster'. It was a clever idea to find a name with simultaneous appeal for intellectuals and food connoisseurs, but for me it was pretentious and gross, as was the food itself, which the adult men ate: the red lobsters and the crabs, made to look like living animals. Maybe one should give the people who eat them some credit for being less hypocritical than those who prefer processed meat, but hypocrisy points to guilt and shame; it bears a small promise to change, while there was no shame on the part of Michael and his German companion. I did not comment on the meal, just tried to pace myself with my grilled courgettes and aubergines, as to avoid the awkwardness of sitting at an empty table. But the German boy did not want to eat anything and the father was unhappy about it. At one point I could sense that he was on the verge of an outburst, which made me realise that our role was to help the father make sure that his veneer of civility would not peel off. I was happy when we completed our mission.

Back in the village, our three favourite cats lied close to each other, as if were waiting for us. I mentioned to Andrew that it would be great to take them to England, but he replied that it would be an act of self-indulgence. With us the cats would grow lazy, fat and lonely; in Crete they were happier, even if they had to fight for survival.

Saturday

It was our last day on Crete. We were leaving in the afternoon and had enough time for a swim and lunch in 'Cochili'. However, the weather had changed overnight, with strong wind, rain and waves taking on an angry appearance, as if wanting to finish the slow agony of the holiday season. There was no way we could swim in such weather and it wasdifficult to even have a stroll in the village. We took our time packing, making sure that what we needed for the journey was not buried in the main luggage. Then we waited for the restaurant to open. The time got later and later every day since we'd arrived, probably in step with the diminishing number of customers. Eventually we noticed from our balcony Dimitris's car arriving, and the whole family making the short distance to the restaurant. Dimitris and Nikolaus walked first, the boy holding on tightly to his father's hand, while trying to jump at the same time. Dimitris's wife followed them carrying a cotton bag and a box, probably the food for the day. We waited half an hour for them to settle and then arrived, announcing that it would be our last meal.

'The last supper,' said Dimitris, smiling, although he seemed to be genuinely sad that we were leaving, telling us that we were his favourite customers of the whole season. I asked him how this season compared to the previous ones and he said that he could not answer – it was the first year he was in charge of 'Cochili'. Everything was thus new to him. I asked him what he did before and he replied that he was a taxi driver and bartender and worked in the hotels. These were always poorly paid and unstable jobs, whose precarity was exacerbated by the fact that Crete was controlled by the mafia. Still, he would carry on in these shitty jobs, if not for having Nikolaus. But it was not easy to have a child in Greece these days: the kindergarten was closed down in the village the same year the boy was born. In the heat of the holiday season he was looked after by his aunt, but this arrangement would not work the following year, as she was leaving for Germany to find a job there. Still, Dimitris finished his story by saying:

'We will survive. I will make it a success, because I want to leave him something and make his life easier than mine. I want to be,' – although normally Dimitris was not short of adjectives, this time he couldn't find the right word. Eventually he said, 'be grand for him.'

'His granddad,said Andrew too quickly to realise that his remark could be offensive.

'Yes, his Grand Dad,'Dimitris replied solemnly.

'You will, for sure,'I said, because there was nothing else to be said. Before we left, Dimitris gave us his business card, asking us to let him know when we would be returning, so he could make sure to have a larger selection of vegan meals for me.

As we waited for a taxi to take us to the airport, we could hear the water being pumped out from the hotel's swimming pool. So, after all, the owner kindly waited with this task till the last day of our stay. She also waved goodbye from the small reception. I noticed that Kuśtyczka was standing next to her. So maybe she was her guardian of sort. At the airport I realised that I failed to learn the name of Dimitris' wife. I asked Michael and Andrew, if they knew, but they didn't.

'Why do you need to collect such useless data,'said Andrew. 'Especially, given that you always complain that you have too much to remember. Keep your world small.'

Several days after our return, I read that there was a storm and flooding in Crete. Several people were killed and many businesses were destroyed. I wondered whether 'Cochili' was affected. From a pile of unsent postcards, small maps and other holiday semi-rubbish, which one is unable to throw away straight after a holiday, I whisked out a card with Dimitris' phone number. I was on the verge of phoning him, but in the end I didn't. What wouldI say if he told me that his restaurant was destroyed, that he was in debt? Should I promise to help him? 'Keep your world small' – I remembered Andrew's words.

May arrived and we made a plan to go for a short trip to Bulgaria for the last week in August, to a resort recommended to me by a friend, whose aunt run a restaurant there. I decided to check how it was rated on Trip Advisor. Then it occurred to me to check 'Cochili'. It was there with almost hundred reviews, some from people who visited the last season. I've read the first one: 'Be careful of the little chap that runs the taverna, he will befriend you, only to find later he's after your money.' The author of these words was German. I don't know if I was more happy to find out that 'Cochili' survived the storm the previous autumn or angrier that some stingy kraut dared to smear its reputation. I added my own super-positive review, thinking that perhaps we should go there again, leaving Bulgaria for another occasion.

Heaven for Prostitutes

I always liked meeting people when travelling, and collecting their stories. But, with the passage of time, it's got difficult. Nowadays the bulk of travellers live out their lives on mobile phones and don't like to be disturbed. People with extra time are seen as losers, so the only conversation one can strike-up without being viewed as eccentric or tragic is with the elderly and destitute, because they cannot remove themselves easily from this world, and do not need to pretend that they are super-busy because nobody would believe them anyway. One of my last such encounters with strangers was in Portugal. I had several business meetings scheduled in different parts of Lisbon over several days, and to avoid stress decided to visit some of the venues beforehand to make sure I could find them when the time came, as I am prone to getting lost, even with google maps. One of the meetings was in a restaurant in the old aquaduct, so called Pink Street. The name was on the account of the road surface being painted pink. Predictably, I could not find it. There was nobody to ask except for two old, strange looking, women; each keeping in her hand an empty plastic bottle and an empty packet of cigarettes. The women wore a lot of make-up, short skirts and tight blouses exposing parts of their breasts. On their feet they had golden trainers, which I took as a compromise between elegance and comfort. The women had shapely bodies, but more wrinkles and age spots on their skin than might be expected from women in their seventies, and one was missing several teeth. I asked them about the restaurant and they showed me where it was, warning that it would not be open till late in the afternoon. They asked me about my nationality, but did not understand my answer, thinking that I came from Holland, rather than Poland. One of them informed me that she had a close relationship with Holland and suggested that we go for a drink to celebrate Portugese-Dutch friendship. Correcting this misunderstanding did not change the situation for her as far as celebration was concerned because, for my country, she also had a special place in her heart thanks to the Polish pope, who was for her the best of all popes, a 'true saint'. On that account I dared to differ, but we did not have time to explore this topic.

I had no desire to drink alcohol, but did not want to offend the helpful souls. Moreover, the southern heat was about to start and hence the need to hide from it. We went to a café on the neighbouring street, where my companions were a familiar presence, as they were greeted by their names, Maria and Teresa. It was a place where one still could smoke without being thrown out of the premises and the women took this opportunity, asking if I could buy them a packet of cigarettes, plus each a coffee and a glass of vodka, which I did. I bought the same for myself, as they swore that this was the best protection against the heat. They were right, at least on this particular day.

It seemed awkward to ask them about their occupation, but Maria saved me embarrassment by saying, 'Sweetie, you know what we do for a living, right?'

'I guess,' I replied trying to avoid sounding like I was judging them, then asked, 'how's the business going?'

'It's a bit quiet at the moment,' said Maria, 'but things should pick when there are more tourists.'

Teresa, who came across as the more reserved, smiled with a sad irony and said, 'There'll never be more tourists. This is the peak of the tourist season. To be honest, things aren't going well, therefore we appreciate your gesture of goodwill.'

Maria, recognising that there was no point keeping up the pretence, added, 'yeah, sweetie. To be honest, you saved us. I don't know how we'd have survived till the evening if you didn't get us a drink.'

'Will you get some customers in the evening?' I asked.

'For sure we will. We offer value for money.'

'Was the business better in the past?' I asked.

'Certainly', said Maria, and started to relate to me what became the story of their lives. It was an exaggerated version, as demonstrated by the fact that Teresa corrected her on numerous occasions. But even without this I would have been able to identify the moments when truth had to give into myth, on account of being too painful. What I learnt was that Maria was fifty-five and Teresa fifty-seven. They came to Lisbon in the early 80s, from neighbouring villages over a hundred kilometres from the capital, seeking work. Because they were pretty, they found employment in the bars, in the same district of Lisbon when I met them. Initially they worked as waitresses and behind the bar. The work itself was hard and it was difficult to earn enough to pay rent and buy clothes and cosmetics they needed for their work. Moreover, Maria had younger siblings, whom she promised to help with money. The worst thing, however, according to Maria, was that the managers always asked them to wear high heels. This is how they got their varicose veins. Maria asked me to inspect them from her feet to the top of her thighs. Like rivers and streams passing through changing regions, some were wide and flat, other narrow and bulky; and those at the top of the legs had many tributaries. They were in almost all shades of the rainbow, with the majority being red and dark purple. 'High heels kills,' said Maria more than once during our conversation. The sentence was not grammatical but, otherwise, made for a good slogan.

Prostitution came as a natural solution to most of their problems: it was better paid, allowed for more free time and required less physical effort. The main downside was that it was precarious work. Till recently, there was no option to go free-lance. The only choice was to join the least demanding pimp and be smart, trying to increase one's wages by hiding some. But it was not easy and Maria lost her first tooth due to being 'too smart'. Another work hazard was to get involved in turf wars and both Maria and Teresa experienced a fair amount of unpleasantness related to that. 'Sex Lisbon' was a postcolonial space, with Portugese, Brazilian and German lords fighting for hegemony. More teeth were lost, not mentioning the loss of income and, on occasion, accommodation. Eventually the Germans got the upper hand, to the displeasure of my friends, as the cultural differences always mattered. When Teresa chipped in the conversation, she mentioned a big German guy, a 'true Nazi', who ran several Lisbon bars and brothels as if they were concentration camps. Prostitutes were also required to wear high heels. When I asked if they had more varicose veins from gastronomy or sex work, they admitted that from the latter. 'Maybe childbirth is more painful than walking the night in uncomfortable shoes, but at least no woman gives birth every night for 35 years,' observed Maria.

'But you don't wear high heels now', I noticed.

'Yeah, because now we make our own rules. These days nobody harasses us. So we live as if in a paradise', laughed Maria, maybe with irony, maybe not.

There were many good things about being a prostitute, such as having regular clients, with whom one could forge friendships, even love. This was the case with Maria's Dutch lover, who used to visit Lisbon regularly for eight years and eventually took her to live in his house in Holland. For Maria the guy was as close to the romantic ideal as a real man could be. Unfortunately, this arrangement did not work as she suffered from homesickness and boredom and, most of all, being separated from Teresa. Their affair reassured her that being with one man was not for her. Both women admitted that they were 'naturals' and if not for the fact that sex work is only a small part of being a prostitute, they would be quite happy. I wanted to learn more about Teresa, but it was difficult to shut down Maria, and Teresa was happy to stay in the background.

Although Maria wanted to focus on the positives, their story was ultimately one of decline. They were hit by the fall of the Berlin Wall, 9/11, world economic crises, Portugal's decline, and finally the digital shift, which cleaned the streets of the brightest girls, leaving there only the veterans armed, like Maria and Teresa, with ancient Nokia bricks in their wrinkled hands. In the meantime many of their friends died of drug overdoses, pimp violence and various illnesses. There seemed no point to ask them about future intentions, as obviously they had no long-term plans.

I paid our bill and left Maria and Teresa 20 Euros to share, for which they thanked me profusely. Afterwards I returned to my hotel in a good mood, happy that I managed to help somebody and have an interesting conversation, although charity always leaves with me a trace of guilt. The next day, when I returned to Pink Street, I saw Maria and Teresa again not far from the place I was to meet somebody else. This time, however, I pretended not to see them as, on this occasion, I didn't want to be distracted. They could also spoil the image of them I had constructed in my mind, and change an encounter I would recall with fondness to one I wish I had walked away from. It occurred to me that these travel meetings only work once. It was a sad thought, adding to the lingering pain of the flimsiness of life, which accompanied me since I hit middle age. But there was no time to ponder on it, as there were already new flimsy things to take care of and my shoes were hurting me, even though they were comfy the previous day.

Carlos and Us

Tony met him during his second morning run on the beach near Puerto Plata. They ran in the opposite directions on the empty beach, crossing each other's paths at half past four in the morning. For the first time, they just looked at each other, not sure whether to acknowledge each other's presence. But the next day the guy stopped and asked Tony where he was from. Tony explained that he was Scottish, but living in England and was on holiday with his family in a nearby resort. Likewise, Tony asked the guy if he was local, to which he replied: 'Yes, you can say so, but this is complicated.'

'Okay,, said Tony and continued running, as he is not particularly social nor has time for complicated things.

But the next day Tony felt compelled to stop running when he met the same guy, as it would be impolite to ignore him. Tony remarked: 'Not many people running here.'

'You are right. People in the Dominican Republic don't run, unless they have to. This is the Third World, after all.'

Tony laughed and they started to talk. He learnt that the guy's name was Carlos and he was, as he put it, a 'public figure'. Yet, the conversation was short, because it was getting warm and Tony was anxious to finish his route without breaking into too much of a sweat. He asked Carlos if he wouldn't mind to continue their exchange in the evening. Carlos didn't mind – he took Tony's phone number and in the evening visited us in our hotel room. Tony had to bring him to the building from the beach side, because the security wouldn't let him enter the resort from the street, while security on the beach was looser.

Over the rest of our stay Carlos kept coming to our hotel almost every day and sat with us on the balcony of our room, drinking slowly piña coladas, which we got for free in one of the several open air cafés in the resort. We preferred to drink our drinks in these cafés, but he didn't like to go there, claiming that he would be identified as a local by the staff and thrown out. We didn't protest, as it would be humiliating for him and for us if something like that happened.

The first day Carlos visited us Alex called him 'ethnically ambiguous'. Indeed, it would be difficult to describe his ethnicity, if we didn't already know it. He had Caucasian features and brown skin, but not exactly Caucasian and not exactly brown. His eyes and nose were similar to Marco from the American series 'Bloodline', who was of Cuban descent, but his cheeks were fuller and his face wider, with a pronounced jaw, similar to Robert Redford, yet he was much shorter than these American actors. He wore a carefully trimmed beard and moustache and his clothes appeared always very fresh, even ironed, rather than taken from a crumpled pile, as it was the case with us. He was slightly hunched and seemed to put more energy into his movements than necessary. My grandmother who knew many Polish Jews from before the Second World War, would describe his posture and movements as Jewish.

At first Carlos looked as if he was in his thirties, but what he was saying suggested that he must have been at least in his mid-forties, to have been able to pack all the experiences he shared with us. There was also a certain fatigue about him, despite his unusual fitness . He came across as a man who was tired of trying, yet not in a position to give up.

Day after day we learnt more about Carlos, but I was never sure if the bits of information he divulged to us were facts or projections, as on several occasions there were inconsistencies. However, I never challenged him, because I didn't want to embarrass him and because his projections were as interesting and truthful to me as his truths. We learnt that he studied law in Harvard and worked in the States for several years in some large firm, before he returned to the Dominican Republic, partly from patriotism and partly because he believed that his chances there were greater. In the States he had to be a follower and an employee; in his country he could be a trailblazer and his own man, as proved by the fact that in the Dominican Republic he was involved in the production of the first Dominican historical cinematic superproduction, a hybrid of a historical epic and a superhero movie. He was also exporting Dominican rum to fifty different countries and stood as a candidate in the parliamentary election. In-between, he lived in Spain for seven years because his second wife was Spanish and his second child was born there.

Currently, he was involved in trading different goods between different countries with partners from the States, Columbia and Mexico. This was a multi-million operation, involving leasing several ships, negotiating with tens of governments and employing hundreds of people. The outcome of the operation was uncertain. If they succeeded, they would become multi-millionaires; if they failed, they would become bankrupt. Tony was laughing when listening to Carlos, partly because it sounded like a story of drug smuggling and partly because it amused him when people strove to be multi-millionaires. He couldn't understand those wishing to transcend middle-classness.

I always thought that a large portfolio career hides a portfolio of failures and this was also what one could gather listening to Carlos, although he never mentioned that he was fired from a job or that his business operation caused a deficit. Rather, his businesses were unfinished or he switched his interests finding better routes to self-fulfillment. The only thing which he admitted was that he lost in the last parliamentary election. On this occasion this was because he stood as an 'independent' and in the Dominican Republic one couldn't be independent in politics. Politics involved dependence – on big business, on clandestine networks of people who already hold power. All Carlos' failures were the fault of others. For example, in Spain he couldn't stay not only because he was, in his heart, Dominican and his marriage disintegrated, but also because for Spaniards he was 'too black'. He said this sporting a white shirt and white cotton trousers, and I wasn't sure if such attire was meant to highlight his dark skin or draw attention away from it.

Carlos' love of his country was a type of love one can find in books of many postcolonial writers and among some successful migrants from Asia and Africa whom I met in Britain. These people seemed to love their countries deeply and liked to talk about it as it was at the core of their identity. However, I couldn't stop thinking that they had to love their countries so ostentatiously to compensate for their lack of commitment, of which the ultimate proof was that they lived abroad and rarely visited their homeland. It was different from the patriotism of Swedes or Danes who didn't care to talk about it, but believed their country was the best in the world and had no desire to leave it. There were moments when Carlos was on the verge of becoming a full-blown postcolonial, in the vein of Jamaica Kincaid, accusing the bloody Spaniards or Americans of screwing the Dominican Republic over and over again.

However, Alex, who was only thirteen then, prevented such an outburst by adopting an unapologetically colonial position. This Carlos found out when he asked Alex whether he would like to live abroad:

'Maybe, but only in the West. The West is the best; it has the highest standard of living and the most developed culture. It is only in the West you can say publicly how bad your country is and get away with it. Try to do this in China or Saudi Arabia. Only western countries don't blame anybody else for their failures and try to repay for the sins of their past, slavery or so on. Did you hear of any descendants of slave owners in Africa who pay reparations to descendants of the slaves?'

Carlos laughed, but did not engage in any discussions with Alex, only turned to us, saying: 'You have a very intelligent child. Beware!'

One could sense that Carlos was entrapped in the Dominican Republic and if an opportunity allowed, he would leave. Perhaps, by this point, he'd run out of opportunities. To this he alluded when he told us that his girlfriend, who was twenty years his junior, lived in Miami, but he couldn't join her as he had these unfinished businesses around Puerto Plata. Yet, as for somebody with a portfolio of jobs, he had a remarkable amount of time, given that he kept visiting us every day and he did so, as he told us, straight from the fitness club, where he spent up to two hours a day. But this surplus of time might have had something to do with the fact that he was insomniac; he only slept in the short intervals between long spans of time of strenuous activity.

Every day when he left we smiled at each other, but rarely said anything. It was only Alex who once said that 'the guy is a fraud,' to which Tony replied that 'somebody who runs at 4 o'clock in the morning cannot be a fraud'.

Carlos was very friendly but I noticed that he looked at us with a mixture of contempt and jealousy. I remembered such a mixture from the 1980s, when I travelled with fellow Poles to India, China and Russia and we met there many westerners, who attracted the same emotion in us. There was contempt, because they seemed to be oblivious to the many opportunities such travels offered, like trading goods between these countries or finding good hotels for pennies, and there was jealousy, because they possessed some things which were unattainable to us, such as better passports and direct access to western currencies. Now we were an object of Carlos' jealousy, because we had better passports and were unambiguously white, while he was 'too black' for certain situations. He treated us with scorn, because we were average, boring middle-class people, who didn't try to do anything adventurous in their lives, as proved by the fact that for a holiday we chose a resort populated by similarly boring, middle-class people. I could see him arriving in our room with a mental grid, ready to place there everything we said. For this purpose, every evening Carlos asked us what we had done that day and Tony responded with his naïve openness and precision.

At the beginning it all worked well, because there were only stories of sea, beach and bad meals. Sometimes Carlos stopped us to find out if anything more interesting had happened that day. I knew that he asked not in hope that such thing happened, but to reassure himself that nothing about our lives fell outside his preconceptions, that our facts adjusted to his theories. However, as the days passed, literally and metaphorically we moved further, and I could see that Carlos grew irritated. It started when we said that we went to Puerto Plata that day and visited an amber museum. Without thinking much, I told Carlos that some years previously I visited an amber museum in Gdansk, where there was a large piece of blue amber and the guide had told me that it was a gift to Poland from the Dominican Republic. I fell in love with this stone and wanted to see more of it, so it was great to get my wish fulfilled. I was immensely pleased to find in the museum of Puerto Plata a large piece of Polish amber, a gift to the Dominican Republic from Poland.

'This is a nice story, but museums never show real life,' Carlos remarked.'

'Of course they don't,' I replied, 'but it is not real life one looks for in the museum of amber.'

Another disappointment for Carlos was the story of my trip to San Domingo. A bus excursion, organised by the tourist office, it was an embodiment of an attraction for the people who needed a guide, because they weren't able to guide themselves. I could see Carlo's eyes sparkle when Tony told him the day before that I was going there, to fill the time when he and Alex went diving. However, I managed to get lost and, as usual, I forgot to take my mobile phone, so I wasn't able to find the tour bus. After waiting over an hour for my arrival, the bus left and I stayed overnight in a shoddy hotel in San Domingo, spending the following day in the city, before catching the only bus back to Puerto Plata. Of course, this trip made Tony and Alex very worried and Tony didn't want to meet Carlos that evening as he was spending the day between the tourist office, which organised the trip and the police station in Puerto Plata, which, instead of reassuring him that it was unlikely that I was mugged, raped or killed, told him that it was very likely that one of these things had happened.

My wife can make an adventure even from her trip to work', said Tony, when we met Carlos after this trip. 'You understand now why we go on holiday to these middle-class concentration camps. She has to be locked or led on a leash, otherwise she gets lost.'

Carlos was laughing, but I sensed his unease because a physical or mental cripple is, by definition, not a tourist; for such a person the most beaten track feels like striding the Amazon rainforest or trekking in the Himalayas.

Carlos suffered the biggest blow when Tony revealed our main reason to visit the Dominican Republic – to see the house where the Austrian singer Falco lived and the place where he died, because I was a Falco fan. Tony explained that the initial plan was to rent Falco's villa, which after his death changed hands several times and eventually was bought by some entrepreneur who was renting it to tourists. However, although we were able to locate it on the internet, renting it from the distance proved impossible; the only option was just to find it. In the tourist office in Puerto Plata we were told that it became part of the holiday village 'Paradise Holiday'. We signed up to tour this village, on the proviso that we would be shown the 'Villa Falco'. A car took us to the village some ten miles from Puerto Plata, where we got into golf carts which took us to the first villa, informing us: 'This is Villa Falco'.

'It isn't,' I said, knowing it from photographs.

'Okay,' he replied and then drove us a bit further, saying again, 'This is Villa Falco,' to which I responded that it wasn't. The situation was repeated maybe twice or three times, by which point we got tired and distressed, as the sterile 'Paradise Holiday' village turned out to be one of the saddest places we ever visited. In the end the driver took us to a villa which was quite a bit larger than the rest and said, 'Okay, maybe this is not Villa Falco, but it is a nice villa. It has a swimming pool and four bedrooms and a bar with free drinks. Take it, you will like it here,' to which Tony replied:

'We are not looking for *a* villa, but *the* villa. Don't you understand the difference?'

'I'm not sure he did,' said Tony to Carlos, 'but he stopped persuading us and dropped us off at a place where we could get a taxi back to the resort. When our ordeal was over, we were immensely happy to be back here.'

'So you travelled all the way from England *not to see* the house of Falco?' asked Carlos with a smirk. 'What a waste of time.'

It wasn't a waste of time for me. On the contrary, I never felt closer to Falco than travelling in a golf cart among the non-descript villas. But there was no point in telling Carlos, as it would break the tacit agreement that we remain tourist attractions for each other: fake or at least decontextualised. The situation might have changed had we visited Carlos in his house because houses are more truthful than people. Carlos told us almost every day that we should visit him in this house, which he half-mockingly described as the most beautiful man-sion this side of Puerto Plata and taste the great Dominican cuisine – the opposite of the food we get in the resort. Yet, he didn't set any date for the visit and we didn't insist, as every day there was enough for us to do. However, when only two days remained until our departure, Tony told Carlos that the next day was the last chance for us to see his house and Carlos promised to fetch us at 6 pm. and take us there in his car. That morning he texted Tony to let him know that he fell ill and had to cancel our visit. We never heard from him again.

The Jewellers of Goa

Although Ada had passed thirty, she was still going on holidays with her parents, in part to keep her teenage brother company and in part because they could afford holidays in far-away countries, while she couldn't. This time they went for a two-weeks trip in one of the coastal resorts in Goa. Ada's parents and her brother found the place much to their taste and in their typical way enjoyed the touristy pleasures: swimming, diving (although this was only for the boys), eating out and feeding cows and other stray animals. To this list Ada's mother added shopping. Every day, after her morning swim, she took her favourite black bag and went to the village, visiting every second shop she was invited to come into, till her black bag was full and she repeated this routine in the afternoon. She also got her hair cut by a local hairdresser and adorned her hand with a henna tattoo. Ada's mother claimed that in this way she killed many birds with one stone: indulged in her love of colour, supported the local economy, solved the problem of buying Christmas presents and learnt about the local culture. Ada was sceptical about the last advantage, but Ada's mother pre-empted her criticism saying: 'I don't strive to be authentic and I don't mind to appropriate their culture, not least because they are happy for me to do it. Let me be postcolonial and I'm okay with you being *woke*.' She must have had a point as after several days of these expeditions, when Ada's mother walked the streets, it felt like the whole village called her by her name. Ada's father looked at his wife's treasure hunt with an indulgent amusement, but he didn't say anything and after some time started to go to the village on his own, with some conspiratorial aura about him.

Most of the shopping time, Ada's mother spent with the jewellers who were also selling scarves, because buying necklaces, bracelets, earrings and pashminas required more time than buying sweets or fruit and there was a certain ritual which needed to be observed to regard transaction as satisfactory. It required drinking tea, bargaining, albeit slightly (heavy bargaining was associated with Russians who had a bad reputation among Goa's merchants) and engaging in lengthy conversations, usually about family matters. The jewellers asked Ada's mother about her job and her family. Most likely this was a way to find out about her purchasing power and whether there was a potential market of female relatives into which they could tap, but perhaps there was also an element of ordinary curiosity. Ada's mother reciprocated by asking them about their families, the places they were from, their culture and their plans. In this way she learnt that all the jewellers came from Kashmir, to which they returned for two months in a year, they were Muslims and usually had large families. The older, who were the minority, had four or five children; the younger were usually single and had three to five siblings. They were all male.

When she told the jewellers that she had a daughter in her early thirties, they asked her to bring her in. She replied that her daughter did not wear jewellery, but they asked her to bring her anyway, for tea and chat, as their lives were boring, especially towards the end of the season when there were few tourists and the day dragged on. As there wasn't much else to do in the village apart from swimming and doing things on her smartphone, after a week Ada decided to accompany her mother shopping. She wanted to go to the shop where her mother bought a black-grey scarf and some papier-mâché ornaments but her mother didn't remember where she purchased these things:

'All the shops and all the vendors are the same to me,' she said.

'This is only because you don't know them.'

'For sure this is the case, but I don't mind if they don't appreciate my uniqueness either. Buying a scarf or a pair of earrings is not necessarily like making love, even if they try to make you feel as if it is. They follow their own rituals and I follow mine.'

The first jewellery shop to which Ada's mother brought her daughter was on the main street, but on its less crowded part, on the right side from their hotel. It was a small detached building with upstairs and downstairs and a strong smell of burning incense. After saying 'hello' Ada's mother left, as she promised to go for a coffee with an English woman whom she met the previous day in their hotel.

The guy who worked there looked as if he was in his thirties. He was short, energetic and – as Ada expected – persuasive: the type who doesn't take 'no' for an answer. As soon as Ada's mother left, he moved from behind his counter and shook her hand:

'My name is Kaushal, which means "smart". What is your name?'

'Ada.'

'What does it mean?'

'I don't know, but probably not "smart".'

The guy laughed in a somewhat forced way.

'I am from Kashmir and everything what I sell here is from Kashmir. Do you know Kashmir?'

'Not really. The only Kashmir I know is the one from Led Zeppelin's song.'

'Sorry, I don't know it,' said Kaushal.

'Don't worry, it's an old song. Even young English people don't know it.'

'Would you like some tea? I have here Kashmir tea, Turkish tea, English tea, Chinese tea.'

'Kashmir tea, please.'

They sat on a mat on the floor with small glasses filled with the hot spicy drink. Ada's mother warned her that the tea would not be to her taste, being too sweet, but actually Ada liked it and when she finished, asked Kaushal for the second helping.

'Do you have a husband?' asked Kaushal, putting some dark sweets on a small plate.

'No,' said Ada.

'A boyfriend?'

'No. What about you?'

'I don't have a wife or a girlfriend either. So maybe I can be your boyfriend?' asked Kaushal.

'I don't think so,' said Ada.

'Why?'

'I'm not looking for a boyfriend.'

'Why not?'

'I have other things on my mind, other issues, other plans. And I want to be free.'

'I cannot believe it,' said the jeweller. 'Young women are always looking for boyfriends, unless they already have one.'

'This is your problem then, if you don't believe me,' said Ada.

For a moment there was a tense silence, after which Kaushal asked: 'Do you want to look at my jewellery?'

'Not really. I don't wear jewellery.'

'Why not?'

'It feels redundant, like a boyfriend.'

'So maybe you want to look at my scarves. They are really beautiful. Some are made of wool, other of silk. My family in Kashmir is making them. You will not find more beautiful scarves in the whole world than those from Kashmir and more beautiful in entire Goa than in my shop.'

'Okay. I will look at them,' said Ada, finishing her tea. 'I rarely wear scarves myself, only one warm black in winter, but I might buy some for my girlfriends.'

'Please do. I will give you a special price, as this is the end of the season and it makes no sense to take them back to Kashmir.'

Kaushal spread many scarves on the counter, saying: 'Please touch them. They feel like skin touching skin.'

'Yes, they are nice,' said Ada, but couldn't make up her mind, as there were too many of them to choose from. But for Kaushal it meant that there were not enough and he piled more on those already spread on the counter.

'Please stop,' said Ada. 'It's enough.'

She quickly took two silk scarves and one pashmina and promised to come another day for tea.

'Just for tea. No obligation to buy anything,' said Kaushal when she was paying him.

'Of course not,' said Ada.

Back in the hotel Ada showed her scarves to her mother, who said that they were indeed beautiful and it would be worth returning to Kaushal's shop to buy more. But it was difficult to find his shop amongst dozens spread out over several streets in the village, especially as Ada didn't pay attention to its name. Thus instead the next day Ada headed to another one, whose proprietor sat on a stool in front of his shop, presumably waiting for customers. When he saw Ada, he said 'Please come in,' and shook her hand as soon as she entered.

Like Kaushal, he was rather short, with dark hair and dark skin and looked as if he was in his early thirties.

'You are not Russian, aren't you?' he asked.

'No. Do I look Russian?'

'Probably you don't, but I want to be sure, as I have no time for Russians. They spend hours going through my stuff without buying anything or offering me prices below my cost.'

'I'm from England. The country of your colonial oppressors.'

He ignored her remark and said:

'We need more English people here, fewer Russians. Why so few English are coming?'

'Maybe due to austerity. The middle classes cannot afford to go to India anymore and the millionaires wouldn't come here. They prefer to be on private islands or private yachts.'

'It's bad,' he said. 'What is your name?'

'Ada'.

'Really? Mine is similar, only longer – Abhinanda, which means joy. We must have something in common.'

'Abhinanda is also a name of a Swedish punk band.'

'I don't know about it. I don't know much about western music. How old are you?'

'Thirty-two', said Ada.

'I'm twenty-six', said Abhinanda. 'Do you have a husband?'

'No. Do you have a wife?'

'No, but my family wants to marry me off when I return home after the tourist season.'

'Are you happy about it?'

'There is nothing to be happy or unhappy about. It is just how things are in Kashmir.'

'Will you bring your wife here?'

'No, I don't think so. Nobody does it.'

'Why not?'

'This job is too hard for women, as it requires staying late at night and utter concentration. One cannot have kids when doing it, because one cannot focus on children and customers at the same time plus the apartment upstairs is too small for a family. It's barely enough for me.'

'What about single women? Wouldn't they be good in the jewellery business?' asked Ada.

'There are no single women in our culture,' he responded. 'It's the men's job to marry off their sisters and daughters and provide for them. But I know in England it is different.'

He was looking at Ada boldly as if he wanted to measure her assets. Although this put her off she didn't want to leave as she was worried that he might turn nasty if she didn't buy anything. So she said: 'Can you show me some earrings?'

He put maybe thirty on the counter and after five minutes or so Ada chose two pairs, knowing that she couldn't do so in haste as buying things quickly would only encourage him to show her more and ultimately force her to buy more.

When she paid, Abhinanda said: 'Now is time for some tea. I will serve you Kashmir tea. It is like a magic potion.'

'Thanks, but no thanks. I must return to the hotel as we go to Panaji in less than an hour.'

'There is nothing to see in Panaji.'

'Perhaps, but we made a decision to go and a taxi will collect us from the hotel.'

'Okay, but come tomorrow, just for tea. Nobody will make such a tea for you like me.'

'Maybe I will come,' said Ada.

'Not maybe, but sure. Promise. The name of my shop is "Hidden Gems"'.

'Promise,' said Ada, although she was thinking that there was no way she would return to this creep.

The next day Ada ventured to the other side of the village, which was less pleasant, because unlike in the other part, where clusters of shops and restaurants were divided by areas of greenery used by cows as their pasture and resting grounds, it was completely built up and full of tacky restaurants with English names. However, she didn't want to risk meeting Abhinanda again.

She entered a shop squeezed between a large stall with clothes and a tailor's, which offered to make a dress or a suit in 24 hours. The two men sitting in front of the shop were so immersed in a conversation that they didn't notice Ada till she asked: 'Which of you is in charge of this shop?'

'It's me,' said one who was slimmer and shorter. The other was rather fat and unusually tall for men Ada saw in Goa.

Without asking, he led Ada to the shop which was pleasantly dark and cool, unlike the jewellery sellers who didn't seem to use air conditioning.

He switched on the light and repeated what the other sellers told her during her previous shopping expeditions: 'All this stuff is from Kashmir. I have jewellery and scarves. I can give you a good price as this is the end of the season.'

Ada thought that this had to be indeed the end of the season as he came across as tired and sleepy. He even had puffy eyes and ruffled, unkempt hair. This made it difficult to assess his age – he could be forty or twenty-five, given that the jewellers in Goa seemed to look older than their real age. Unlike the previous men, he didn't ogle her, which made for a pleasant change and there was a certain touching shyness and clumsiness about him. She was thinking that it was good that he wasn't selling china as he would destroy half of his ware.

Unfortunately, his stuff seemed to be of a lower standard than in the shops Ada visited previously. Everything seemed to be mass produced and pashminas weren't even packed each piece separately, but made a large and rather disorderly pile, on top of which there were two bowls with some unfinished food.

'These look nice,' said Ada, as she felt sorry for the guy. 'Is your family producing them?'

'Some, but mostly we collect stuff made by other people in our village and pay them when the ware is sold.'

'Do you choose it yourself?'

'Until recently it was mostly my father, but from next season I will do it myself.'

Ada went through the stack of pashminas and eventually chose one.

'Get a second one and I will sell it to you half price. Also, if you buy a necklace, you get earrings free. By the way, would you like a cup of tea? I will make some for myself. I have here English tea, Russian tea and Kashmir tea.'

'Kashmir tea, please,' said Ada, browsing through boxes of earrings and necklaces. Eventually she chose some simply because they looked better than the others.

'I will take those. Do you also have Christmas decorations made of papier-mâché? My mother bought some yesterday and I really liked them.'

'No, I don't have them here, but I can get them for you for tomorrow,' said the man. 'My friend sells them in his shop in another part of the village.'

'No need, I can buy them elsewhere, I was simply curious.'

He put a teapot on the floor and brought two china cups. When they started to drink, he asked her:

'What is your name?'

'Ada'.

'Mine is Tahir.'

'Does it mean something?'

'Yes, "pure". Are you married?' asked Tahir.

'No. What about you? Are you married?'

'You can say so,' said Tahir.

'What is s that meant to mean?' asked Ada.

'I was married to a woman last year, but I don't consider her to be my true wife.'

'Why so?'

'She is sick. She suffers from epilepsy and other illnesses. And she is a stranger to me; we have nothing in common. I didn't want to marry her, but my father and her father were close friends and my father promised that he would marry his oldest son to his daughter. He wanted to ensure that it happened before he died and so there was a wedding last year, because by then my father was very sick. Now my father is dead so I want divorce her.'

'It sounds rather complicated. Wouldn't it be better to refuse a marriage than to agree to go through with it and then plot a divorce?'

'No, in our culture it doesn't work like that. The marriage means that she will be looked after by my family, even if we don't live together. She is currently living with my mother and my sisters.'

'Can't you bring her here so you get to know each other better?'

'No, there will be nothing for her here. Most of the time I'm downstairs with the customers and she has to be always with somebody, in case she has a fit. If this happens, I might not hear her and she might die before she gets help. I keep thinking about the whole situation and I cannot sleep. I go to bed late, but wake up after two hours thinking about how unlucky I am: trapped here, in the shop; trapped in Kashmir, when I'm home.'

'Things might be better, when you divorce,' said Ada, half-asking, half-stating.

'Perhaps, but then I will be on my own for the rest of my life. I don't want to marry any girl from my village. They don't suit me and those from Goa, who are Hindu, don't talk to us. They don't like Muslims here. It is only tourists who are friendly to people like me.'

'So sad. Looks like you will stay "Tahir" by name and by destination,' said Ada. She felt moved by his story, but at the same time was barely able to suppress giggling.

'Do you have a free evening?' asked Tahir. 'We can go to a restaurant or a disco. I will pay for you.'

'Thanks, but this evening I go with my parents and my brother to the night market.'

'There is nothing special in this market and the prices are higher than here,' said Tahir.

'Perhaps you are right, but we made a decision to go and a taxi is already booked for 6 p.m.'

'So maybe you can come tomorrow. I normally close the shop at 11 but can close it earlier if you want to go somewhere. Almost nobody comes these days anyway, as this is the end of the season and most tourists already have left. Only Russians are coming in, but they are a waste of time.'

'Perhaps, but don't wait for me.'

'I will wait for you,' said Tahir. 'Tomorrow and the following day. And this is my present for you.' – he gave her a bracelet with red and blue stones.

'I cannot take it like that. I will pay for it.'

'No, keep it,' said Tahir, putting it in a bag. 'I also put in-side a card with my address and the name of the shop, "Tahir's Jewels", in case you forget where it is, although it is easy to find.'

At the night market Ada and her mother bought so much jewellery, scarves, clothes and bric-a-brac that they vowed not to buy any more, ever. However, the following day her father and brother went diving and Ada's mother went somewhere with her new circle of English friends and Ada didn't have much to do except for scrolling through her smartphone, which she didn't want to do during the last days of her stay in Goa. So she took a stroll into the village, aware that even-tually she would end up in one of the jewellery shops. Yet she somehow managed to navigate in such a way that she omitted all the shops she visited before, largely by taking side streets, where there weren't many shops. Eventually she found herself standing in front of a shop at the end of the street which led into a nowhere land, covered with weeds and cows' dung. It was practically the last shop in the village and Ada was curious who owned such a place. Apart from being so far off, it didn't look any different from the other jewellery shops, with a vending area downstairs and a small flat upstairs, where supposedly the proprietor lived. Its name was simply 'Kashmir.' Ada walked in, but the light was switched off and there seemed to be nobody there. She shouted: 'Hi, anybody there?'

There was still silence and only when she was about to leave, somebody descended the stairs, showing his bare, large feet and then the rest of his body. The man had black hair and dark eyes, but he looked somewhat different from the jewel-lers whom she met previously. He was taller, had lighter skin, his clothes were looser and he wore them differently, kind of nonchalantly, like an art-college student. He looked gorgeous.

Ada hadn't seen such a handsome man in Goa. Actually, she hadn't seen such a handsome man for ages.

'Hi,' he said as he moved behind the counter, rubbing his eyes, as if he had just woken up. 'How can I help you?' he asked.

Ada noticed that he didn't sound like the other jewellers from Goa. He sounded almost English.

'Hi,' said Ada. 'I guess you are a jeweller from Kashmir.'

'You could say so,' said the man.

'Do you mean you are not really from Kashmir?'

'My father is from Kashmir, but my mother was Dutch.'

'Was?'

'Yes, she passed away several years ago.'

'Oh', said Ada. 'How interesting.'

'Do you want to buy something?' he asked, somewhat abruptly.

'Well, I'm not particularly into ethnic jewellery, but I got a habit of visiting the jewellery shops in the village and I got a small collection of scarves, necklaces and earrings, all special price,' said Ada.

She tried to be sophisticated as she sensed that he was sophisticated too, but he seemed not to notice her efforts.

Instead, he said: 'I have all these things here; my family is making them themselves. Do you want to peruse?'

'Yes, please.'

'First jewellery or scarves?'

'Scarves, please.'

She was waiting for an offer of Kashmir tea, but there was none, so when he put a tall pile of scarves on the counter, she asked him:

'Can you make me some Kashmir tea, please?'

'I don't drink Kashmir tea. In fact, I don't drink any tea at all. But if you are thirsty, I can pour you a glass of water.'

'Yes, please,' said Ada, although she wasn't really thirsty and everywhere she went she carried a bottle with her which she filled before leaving the hotel.

When he went upstairs to bring her water, Ada looked at the jewellery hanging on the wall behind the counter and thought that some of it was nicer than in the other shops: lighter, subtler, more stylish, although still too colourful for her. But she decided that she would buy something, and not for her friends, but for herself as maybe her mother is right that one needs some colour, especially if one lives in England. She also noticed a guitar propped against the wall in the corner.

'Do you work here on your own?' she asked, when he returned.

'Yes.'

'No wife, no girlfriend?' she asked.

'No.'

'So it must feel lonely here, all by yourself,' said Ada.

'Did you come here to enquire about my psychological wellbeing or to buy my stuff?' he asked.

'Sorry. Over the last week I visited many shops like yours and everybody there introduced himself, offered me Kashmir tea and told me about their family history and their loneliness, so I was just surprised that you don't go through the usual ritual,' said Ada.

'Maybe because I'm just new to the job. I only started it this year and I'm still learning the ropes. Or maybe I don't like to talk about myself.'

'I understand. What is your name?'

'Markus.'

'Pleased to meet you, Markus. My name is Ada. You have nice things here,' said Ada, putting aside two pashminas and pointing to a necklace hanging on the wall. 'I will take it too.'

'Do you want to try it?' asked Markus.

'No, I will just take it.'

She was waiting for him to offer her a second necklace or earrings half price, but he didn't. Neither did he put the necklace in a nice hand-made cloth bag, but only in a small plastic one and handed it to her. It was time to go but she couldn't force herself to leave. She also felt as if he wanted her to stay, but was too shy or proud to say so. So she asked:

'Didn't it occur to you to give your shop a fancier name?'

'Actually, I thought it was pretty fancy. It's the title of a Led Zeppelin song. I think the song is great. Do you know it?'

'Yes, I do, although I'm not into that kind of music.'

'What you mean?'

'I don't like rock, especially prog rock. I find it old-fashioned, macho and pompous.'

'Oh,' said Markus. 'For me it is not old-fashioned. I wish I could play as well as Jimmy Page.'

'Have you tried?'

'Yes, I was studying music for a while, in Amsterdam and in London.'

'Why did you return to Kashmir?'

'My mother died. I had no proper job and no money. There were few opportunities for me in Amsterdam and my father wanted me back in Kashmir. I'm his only son and I have two sisters.'

'How interesting,' said Ada. 'I would like to learn more about it,'

'Maybe another time,' said Markus.

Ada felt a small pain in her heart, but continued: 'Can I come another day?'

'Yes, of course you can. This is a shop. The more customers, the better.'

'Maybe we can go out tomorrow evening, when you finish your work?' asked Ada.

'Maybe, but not tomorrow or the day after, as tomorrow I have to go to Mumbai. I can text you when I return.'

'Yes, this will be good.'

When Ada returned to the hotel, she didn't go straight to her room, but to the reception asking whether they would have free rooms after their planned departure. They had and offered Ada a special price as this was the end of the season – it was in fact less than half of what her parents paid for their accommodation. She didn't even need to change her room. When she met her mother Ada said:

'I decided to stay here longer. It will be a pity to return home only after two weeks, given that I haven't seen much of India or even Goa. I can go from here to Mumbai or Delhi and fly to Manchester from there. Besides, I don't need to be in Manchester to do my work.'

'Do as you please, but do you have money to pay for the hotel and everything?' asked Ada's mother.

'Yes.'

'What if you run out of money?'

'I won't. And if I do, I know whom to ask for assistance.'

In the evening Ada helped her brother pack his suitcase. It was light, so she added to it all her shopping. Then she went to her parents' room, where her father proudly showed her and Ada's mother three suits ordered from the local tailor; two were dark grey and one was black.

'These two will keep me going until my retirement. The black will be for funerals, including my own, so you don't need to spend extra on my clothing,' said Ada's father.

'Good thinking,' said Ada's mother. 'Now wait.' She went to the bathroom and when she returned wore a tight red and green dress, which looked very good on her:

'Also made here, but by a different tailor. And I got a second one, half-price.'

They all laughed.

In the morning Ada's mother came to Ada's room with an envelope: 'Here is the cash I haven't used. It should be enough for the return plane from Mumbai or Delhi in case you need it. Try not to lose it.'

A couple of hours later Ada waved her family goodbye. Then she went for breakfast, had a swim in the sea and went for a stroll in the village.

The Scarves from Candolim

From my holiday in Candolim in India I brought home fifteen scarves. They were sold to me by Lisa, a beach vendor, working on a strip of beach belonging to our hotel. Her other job was to help a guy running a fast food shack, which doubled up as the deckchairs' rental. In exchange for working for him, she was allowed to trade on his patch and receive a 'free' lunch, typically what was not sold that day. Every day Lisa started her job at 8.30 a.m. and finished at 6.30-7.00 p.m.

Some time ago I discovered that holidaymakers have three approaches to beach vendors. The first type regard them as pests, which one has to endure on holidays, like mosquitos or sand in one's bed. These people ask the vendors to go away and in extreme cases complain to the authorities about being harassed by them. The second type enjoys their presence and keeps buying stuff from them, seeing it as a bargain or a distraction from long unadventurous hours spent on the deckchairs. The third type regards buying their fare as a form of charity. These types are not exclusive and during the course of two weeks a holidaymaker can make the journey from one type to another and back. For example, too many vendors coming to one's deckchair offering a foot massage or an ankle chain would eventually annoy the most charitable or bargain-oriented holidaymaker. And conversely, spotting something interesting in the hand of a vendor or on the deck-chair of a neighbour might change the most aloof holiday-maker into a magpie, suddenly browsing through the pile of scarves, jewellery or colourful bags with sparkling eyes.

On this holiday the first type overshadowed the two remaining ones. It consisted mostly of Russians, who never bought anything on the beach and rarely rented the deckchairs, on the account of being stingy beyond repair. At least, this is what the locals said about them. Some British people were also in this category, although, unlike the Russians, they were typi-cally very polite. Then there were Indians. They also didn't buy anything, as they knew the true value of the stuff peddled to tourists, yet they were better than the Russians as occasionally they paid for massages or pedicures.

A plump middle-aged couple from Halifax fitted best the second category. They were adamant not to leave the beach be-tween 10 a.m. and 5 p.m., because their hotel was too far away to walk from there more than once a day. They also admitted that wherever they went, they did not venture outside the re-sort – the sun and the sea was everything they desired and were prepared to pay for. These beach lovers, inevitably, took all their meals, typically fish and chips and macaroni cheese, in the shack, and made all their shopping on the beach. By the time their holiday was coming to the end, the husband had six pairs of shorts and two shirts, and the wife eight dresses and three scarves. Each also got about ten massages. From the per-spective of the beach vendors, they were the perfect customers, because everything they bought on the beach seemed like a bargain for them, as they compared it only with the British prices. They were also a decent folk, as on top of giving the beach vendors much needed custom, they left them all their remaining cosmetics and everything which they didn't need in their luggage, also feeding a stray dog who throughout their stay slept under their deckchair.

The third category was represented by a woman from London called Ann, who'd been coming to Candolim with her husband every year for the last four years, always staying in the same hotel. She was in her early fifties, but had a slim and athletic body, the most beautiful swimming costume on the beach and make-up which didn't melt in the sun. None of this, however, impressed her husband who was always sleeping with his back turned to her. After being in Cadolim four times already, Ann didn't need more stuff from there and she looked too posh to wear cheap scarves from the beach. Yet, she kept buying them and tipping Lisa 200 or 300 Rupees per day for small favours, such as bringing drinks from the shack.

I came somewhere between these two types. I kept buying Lisa's scarves because I liked them, but also because I wanted her to earn something every day. The price we agreed on the first day was 500 Rupees. It was significantly below 750 which she asked for at the beginning, but above 300-400 Rupees, which was her average price. In the end she revealed to me that she bought them for 100 Rupees or less per item. Her profit was thus very high, yet her earnings were small. One problem was that Lisa did not sell many of them. This was because on any given day there were at maximum forty people on her patch of the beach, of whom twenty or more were Indians and Russians. Half of the remaining people didn't want to buy anything either, and half of the rest had already bought scarves from Lisa and therefore had to be pressed hard to buy something else from her. This meant that on an average day there were at maximum five potential customers, whom she had a realistic chance to woo to her fare. Sometimes she succeeded with three or four customers, selling them as many as ten scarves – that was a very good day. But there were also days when she only sold one scarf or nothing. Her profit was reduced also because she had to pay two types of 'taxes' – to the police, who cruised the beach in their jeep, threatening the beach vendors with confiscating their merchandise, and the tax collector, who kept them for himself. On average, one third of Lisa's profit went on bribes or tributes, and at the peak of the tourist season, in January and February, there were weeks when she had to pay these men as much as half of her earnings.

It was not just the pretty scarves which drew my attention to Lisa. Another reason was her appearance and manners – she came across as very different to those haggard Indian women who were pacing the beach with a solemn expression, as if posing for a photographer from 'National Geographic' or Oxfam. Lisa was much shorter, younger and more energetic than them and she wore a baseball cap, which gave her a boyish and mischievous look, although for her it was just protection against the sun. Her jewellery was very modest, as for Indian standards: gold earrings, one gold necklace and one gold stud in her nose. There was a certain elegant simplicity to her saris. Almost every day she wore one in a different colour – peach, dark red, sea green, blue, purple, yellow, with matching trousers. Lisa's face didn't look completely Indian to me, but maybe it was because I studied it more carefully than any other face I saw in India. Her skin was of two colours: a dark shade covered her nose and higher parts of her checks; a paler shade the rest of her face, which gave an impression that the foreground and background changed their places. Later she showed me her pictures taken during the Monsoon season, when her skin was almost pale. Her nose was also adorned with freckles, which added to her mischievous appearance. When she took off her cap, one could see black hair tied up into a neat bun. Unlike the other vendors, Lisa spoke good English, and one which was easier to understand than those of the educated Indians, because she learnt it mostly on the beach, talking to her customers. She wasn't humble when dealing with them and, after a transaction, would shake their hand, something which normally only the male sellers and those who had their own shops did. Her handshake was firm, almost masculine.

We started talking properly when Lisa asked me where I was from. I knew it was only a professional question, whose purpose was to assess my willingness to buy her merchandise and my spending power, but I felt obliged to reciprocate by asking her the same question. She replied that she was from a village in the state of Maharashtra, not far from Mumbai. Some hours after I bought three scarves from her, she returned to occupy the deckchair freed by my son, saying: 'Don't worry, I will not sell you more, just wanted to lie down here for a while, as my back is hurting.' She fell asleep immediately and the bundle of scarves fell on the sand. I collected them and tried to fold them on my deckchair, putting my bag on them so that the wind would not blow them away. If that didn't happen, she probably would have remained another anonymous passenger in my life.

The next day we continued talking and doing business. Every scarf meant buying a piece of the story of Lisa's life. She shared it gladly because most of the day there wasn't much to do – boredom was her worst job hazard; to the heat she was accustomed. Sometimes I couldn't fully understand what she said; sometimes it was obvious that she exaggerated for stronger effect, but I didn't mind, knowing that lies are often more truthful than facts. On occasion Lisa gave me two versions of the same story; the second being a marker of intimacy.

During our first conversation I learnt that Lisa was almost twenty-eight and she was the oldest of five siblings. She had two sisters and two brothers. Her father died of stroke; her mother, who was fifty, lived with Lisa. Although she was the oldest of the girls from her family, she was the only one who wasn't married. Each of her sisters had already two sons. During the holiday season in Goa, which lasted nine months, she lived with her two brothers and her mother in a village a fifteen minute bus ride away from Candolim. They rented a room with a small kitchen. Her brothers were also working in Candolim, each helping in a shop, earning meagre wages; six and seven thousand Rupees respectively per month. Lisa was the main breadwinner in her family; she earned more per day by selling one scarf than any of her brothers. She was also the trailblazer; she was the first from her family to go to Goa, coming ten years previously. She was followed by her older brother, who came to Candolim five years after her and her younger brother, who came for the first time two years previously, bringing their mother with him. Neither of them spoke English, therefore they couldn't sell anything to tourists and Lisa's mother wasn't able to find any paid employment, even sweeping the roads or collecting plastic; there was too much competition in Candolim even for the worst of jobs. Moreover, she wasn't really fit to work; her hip was bad, so she couldn't walk or stand for long.

It took Lisa over a week to confess that in fact she was also already married. It happened when she was sixteen. Her husband was thirty-five and he was already married twice, and mistreated his previous spouses. Asked why she married him, she responded that she had no choice. Her mother wanted to marry her as early as possible and with such a 'weak background', as she kept repeating, she had no chance of getting a better husband, because better husbands demand big dowries and her family couldn't afford it. Lisa knew that her husband was no good, so she ran away from him. For that, she was beaten by her mother so badly that she couldn't get up from bed for days. Was it difficult to forgive her mother for such a brutality? 'No', she replied. Her mother wasn't guilty. It was tradition and politics which were guilty. The government could ensure that the poor families didn't have to pay dowries and make certain things free for the poor. Instead, the poor had to pay disproportionally more for everything.

Luckily, Lisa's marriage was only a village marriage, without registration, so officially she was not married. But in her village she had no future. Even with the husband she had no prospects, because there was little work there – the only work available was on the fields, and it was poorly paid – 50 Rupees per day to children, 100 Rupees to the adults. It had improved since then and presently the adults were paid up to 150 Rupees per day, but this was not money one could live on – it was barely enough to buy food. But one had to work on the fields and send children to work, because without work there was no food and the poor were dying of hunger. Therefore Lisa headed to Goa: the land of opportunities, the West of the East. Once there, first she babysat for a wealthy family, being paid by free food and lodging. It was there that for the first time in her life she got enough food. The result was that she gained ten kilos in one year and became fat. 'Poor people are not used to handling food or money,' she said. 'They don't know how to save it; they gobble everything on the spot.' Later she explained that this might also be the reason Indians eat everything with their hands; the use of a spoon or fork prolongs the distance to quenching one's appetite and frustrates them. From babysitting Lisa moved to a tourist shop. There she picked up the first English words. I asked her what they were and she said, 'Thank you, please come again.' From the shop, she moved to the beach, which was seven years ago. There she adopted her English name – 'my stage name', as she put it half-jokingly; her real name was Rishna.

In step with learning about Lisa's life, my taste in her scarves was changing. During the first days of our acquaintance I was buying some 'traditional' scarves, usually with pictures of elephants against a shiny background, assuming that I wouldn't wear them myself, but they would be good as 'traditional presents from' to all my female friends who also give me 'traditional presents from' in the knowledge that they would most likely be discarded or put aside. But after four or five days of trading, I started to look more closely at her merchandise and when I had trouble finding something I liked, she promised to bring a scarf more to my taste the following day. Those I always liked, maybe because they had a specific address or because I never saw similar ones at the stalls of the street vendors. One, with large owls in yellow, pink, blue and red with a dark-blue background, reminded me of the cover of the Beatles' 'Sgt. Pepper's'. Another one, with patches of colour against a black background, according to Lisa, showed what one sees when one closes one's eyes. 'Your scarves are about dreams,' she said, perhaps to flatter me. 'And they cannot be Indian or Polish English. They have to be,' – she lacked words, so I added 'otherworldly.'

Truth be told, Lisa had more to offer to her customers than scarves. She also had small bags and pieces of jewellery. They, however, didn't sell well, so she mostly kept them buried under the pile of old mattresses near the beach shack and rarely showed to the customers. She also offered tourists small cosmetic jobs, such as massages, pedicures and henna tattoos. But, apart from the first day, she didn't offer theses services to me. There was a tacit agreement between us that she wouldn't increase my white guilt and I wouldn't diminish her postcolonial suffering, and most of the time we observed this rule.

Lisa often said that her life had no future, because in India one is condemned to misery without a husband, or capital, or education. The beach was her trap and her doom. On one side, she was entrapped by the sea; on the other side, by the hotel. She could not venture into its territory, because there was always a uniformed man guarding it and people there would see her more as a pest than those on the beach. Nature and culture were equally powerful in keeping her in her place.

'What about your mobile phone? Doesn't it take you to different worlds?' I asked.

'What worlds? There are no worlds in mobile phones,' she said, somewhat angry. as if I tried to undermine her suffering, so I left it there.

However, one day she herself returned to this topic, telling me that in fact there is a slight chance to improve her lot. The obvious way was by earning more money. This could be achieved either by moving to a better profession or by finding a more attractive merchandise. If she was able to save twice as much as now, in two-three years she would be able to buy a little plot of land to build her own house. It would be a miniature house, with one room or two, but her own. She could have a place to put her clothes, have her own crockery and cutlery, decorate it in her own style. Things might be better if she was able to read and write fluently in English. In this way maybe she would be able to sell things online or at least respond to adverts. Presently, she could write and read, but very little. I suggested that we use the remaining time for reading together and we did so over two days, but after that Lisa asked me to stop teaching her. This was because she had more work in the shack as one of the helpers left and the other got ill and her boss didn't look kindly on her extra activities.

As the holiday season was approaching its end, there were fewer and fewer people on the beach and Lisa's business got worse, while the police jeep kept appearing more often. This affected Lisa's mood. 'You see, my life is hopeless,' she kept saying. 'How can I do business, if everything conspires against me?' I decided to help her by tapping into the last available resource which came to my mind, namely people occupying the hotel's pool area. In terms of fitness and mobility, these poolside holidaymakers are much worse that the beach ones, as upon reaching their loungers and getting their fill of mo-jitos and pina coladas, they get a demented look, which might put off the toughest of merchants. Still, I decided to try by approaching two groups of females, one British, one Amer-ican, showing them the best of my scarves. I pointed out to the first group that buying scarves from Lisa means getting two goods for the price of one: buying cheaply beautiful local creations, produced by blind women (this was most likely a lie, but I noticed that several shops in Candolim promoted themselves in this way) and atoning for the colonial sins of their ancestors. For a stronger effect, I also reminded them of the recent scandals in the British charity sectors, which showed that it was better to help people directly on the ground than to pay the NGOs 'middle men'. The other group I targeted by drawing their attention to the fact that women are squeezed from the best jobs in the tourist sector in Cadolim, with all jewellery and tailor shops run by men, with women reduced to selling cheap souvenirs. They thanked me for opening their eyes to the extent of patriarchy in India, a position which they sympathised with, knowing it well from American university campuses. I didn't see these women again, either at the beach or the pool, so I couldn't check if they brought anything from Lisa, but she claimed that some new women came from our hotel and bought several scarves from her. One of them also paid her for a henna tattoo, which was bringing Lisa more money than selling scarves at this point of the season.

Eventually came the last day of my holiday. I had my last swim in the sea, bought my last scarf from Lisa and had the last conversation with her. She asked me if I would come to Candolim next year and I said that possibly, although it was unlikely I would return, as we couldn't afford such holidays more than once in two-three years and every time we travelled, we wanted to show more of the world to our children.

About the Author

Ewa Mazierska is historian of film and popular music, who writes short stories in her spare time. She published over thirty of short stories in 'The Longshot Island', 'The Adelaide Magazine', 'The Fiction Pool', 'Literally Stories', 'Ragazine', 'BlazeVox', 'Red Fez', 'Away', 'The Bangalore Review', 'Shark Reef', 'Queen Mob's Teahouse' and 'Mystery Tribune', among others. Ewa is a Pushcart nominee and her stories were shortlisted in several competitions, including Exeter short story competition and Ink Tears. She was born in Poland, but from mid-1990s lives in Lancashire, UK, with her husband and a teenage son. Most of Mazierska's stories are inspired by her village of Kowal in the Kujawy region of Poland and by her travels for pleasure and for work. In her professional life she is Professor of Film Studies, at the University of Central Lancashire. She published over thirty monographs and edited collections on film and popular music. They include *Popular Viennese Electronic Music, 1990-2015: A Cultural History* (Routledge: 2019), *Poland Daily: Economy, Work, Consumption and Social Class in Polish Cinema* (Berghahn, 2017) and *Popular Music in Eastern Europe: Breaking the Cold War Paradigm* (Palgrave, 2016), as well as monographs of Roman Polanski and Nanni Moretti. Mazierska's academic work was translated into over twenty languages. She is principal editor of Routledge journal, *Studies in Eastern European Cinema*.

www.ingramcontent.com/pod-product-compliance
Lightning Source LLC
Chambersburg PA
CBHW020021030726

47499CB00007B/2219